MW01132272

SURVIVAL

Karen Cino

Women's Fiction

Survival
3

Mandolay Press

4
Karen Cino

ABOUT THE E-BOOK YOU HAVE PURCHASED:
Your non-refundable purchase of this e-book allows you to only ONE LEGAL copy for your own personal reading on your own personal computer or device. **You do not have resell or distribution rights without the prior written permission of both the publisher and the copyright owner of this book.** This book cannot be copied in any format, sold, or otherwise transferred from your computer to another through upload to a file sharing peer to peer program, for free or for a fee, or as a prize in any contest. Such action is illegal and in violation of the U.S. Copyright Law. Distribution of this e-book, in whole or in part, online, offline, in print or in any way or any other method currently known or yet to be invented, is forbidden. If you do not want this book anymore, you must delete it from your computer.

WARNING: The unauthorized reproduction or distribution of this copyrighted work is illegal. Criminal copyright infringement, including infringement without monetary gain, is investigated by the FBI and is punishable by up to 5 years in federal prison and a fine of $250,000.

A Mandolay Press Book

Women's Fiction

Mystical Wonders: Survival

E-book ISBN: 9781519743466

First E-book Publication: April 2014

Second Edition: December 2015

Cover design by Karen Cino

Edited by Stephanie Balistreri

Proofread by M.S. Daniels

PUBLISHER

Mandolay Press

Dedication

Survival is dedicated to all the victims of Hurricane Sandy in Staten Island, New York.

Acknowledgement

I like to thank my editor, Stephanie Balistreri. She's the best! A special thanks to my mom and dad who continue to support me through my journey, along with my adult kids, Michael and Nicole. My writing friends, Tanya Goodwin, Carolyn Gibbs, Jean Joachim and Cathy Greenfeder who always help me work through the rough spots in my story. I also like to thank my friends, Liz Galiano, Nancy Miceli, Diane Reems and Barbara Sarnelli for their continual support of my dreams. Dreams do come true.

<u>Other Books by Karen Cino</u>

Roses

The Boardwalk

Circle of Friends (Book 1)

Second Chances (Book 2)

The Right Call (Book 3)

Survival (Book 4)

Love Challenges and Desires

SURVIVAL

Karen Cino
Copyright © 2014

Chapter One

The day started out just like any other. Madison stood on her back porch in a heavy red sweater, leaning her elbows along the railing, admiring the foliage. This time of the day had always been her favorite.

Everything had been going wonderfully between her and Dino. Even though the physical side of their relationship had been challenging, the emotional side had become rock solid. Starting Rockin' Magazine had been the best idea she'd ever had. They worked together at least eight hours a day on the magazine, never arguing while working through any disagreements. The experience brought them closer, making the emotional process of healing after his heart attack much more bearable.

Today, she decided she needed to speak to him about last night. He had tried so hard to keep his erection, but sadly failed. The upside had been his ability to get an erection, the first one since his heart attack and open-heart surgery. Something within led her to believe today would be the turning point in their lives.

This morning, she could smell the scent of the ocean as the wind blew from east to west onto her porch. Madison couldn't wait for Dino to wake up. Last night had been wonderful. Even though they hadn't made love, the intimacy of their foreplay had brought her to orgasm. She would tell him this, letting him know what they had shared left her with a feeling of peace.

Just as she turned to go into the house, the roaring of sirens filled the air. A few minutes later, she smelled smoke. The fire had to be close as the distant sound of the sirens became louder.

After walking down the back steps, she took the red and beige brick path along the side of her house to the front. Madison opened the six foot white gate. Immediately, she saw smoke coming from what looked like a half mile away. The thickness of the gray plumes blended into the now darkened sky. Funny, how the weather changed in a matter of minutes.

Madison walked into the house, closing the front door behind her. Another strong cup of coffee would be exactly what she needed on such a brisk day. Glancing at the digital clock on her stainless steel stove, she still had some time to get breakfast together before Dino got up.

Turning the gas on under the frying pan, she made French toast with eggbeaters and whole wheat bread.

"I'm smelling something real good," Dino said.

"French toast." Madison turned to face him. "You're up early."

"I couldn't sleep. I kept thinking about last night."

Madison poured him coffee before placing his dish on the table. "So have I. Last night felt like a dream. You made me feel so good."

Dino walked over to Madison and wrapped his arms around her waist. "I feel things are going to get better."

Taking her hand in his, he slid it down his pajama pants. Immediately, Madison felt his erection. Raising her gaze to his, she grinned. "I'm sure you can read my mind."

Smiling back, Dino lifted her into his arms. Madison wrapped her legs around his waist while taking his head in her hands, kissing his lips, forehead and neck. As Dino carried her into the living room her cell phone rang.

"Ignore it," she said.

Dino continued up the stairs. "I am."

"Whatever happens once we get upstairs, I want you to know I love you so much."

Placing her down on the bed, he kissed her lips, then scattered kisses down her neck. The sensation electrified her limbs. Opening her sweater, he pushed it off her shoulders, along with her T-shirt. As his lips dropped to her breasts, the landline rang. Neither one of them budged until they heard Heather screaming for help on the answering machine.

They both jumped up. Madison punched her phone number into the phone. The first time she got a busy signal. She continued to keep calling until the phone rang.

"Heather, it's Aunt Madison. What's wrong?"

"It's the store. It's on fire. I already called 911. Please come."

"I'll be right there."

Madison hung up the phone. "Dino, Fay's shop is on fire. We got to get there. Heather is hysterical."

"How? When?" Dino asked sliding on his jeans.

"I don't know. I couldn't understand her." Madison twirled around in her sneakers, pointing to his black boxers on the floor. "What, are you going commando?"

"Apparently so." He lifted his cell phone. "Want me to call Shari?"

"Yes." Madison slid her sweat shirt over her shirt. "Tell her to meet us there."

* * * *

Shari arrived first. Thomas always woke up at six-thirty every morning. She had just dropped him off at school when her cell phone rang. As she pulled up, the firemen were already trying their best to put out the three-alarm fire. The police had already put up the yellow tape to keep the crowd across the street.

"Aunt Shari."

Shari turned around when she heard Heather scream her name. Opening her arms, Heather fell into them. "Are you all right?"

"Yes. If I didn't go get coffee across the street, I would have been in there," she cried. Heather stepped out of Shari's arms pointing to the diner. "Being twenty minutes late getting my latte with extra whipped cream saved my life."

"Thank God for those extra calories. You're right, they saved your life."

Shari turned when she heard Madison call her name. "I'm over here." Shari waved as Madison and Dino approached her.

Madison quickly hugged her, before embracing Heather.

"Are you all right?" Madison stepped back, looking at Heather. "What happened? When? Why?"

"I don't know Aunt Madison. Like I told Aunt Shari, I went into the diner for a latte. When I came out, I saw the flames coming out of the side of the building."

Madison looked up to the sky. "Your grandfather was watching over you. You never drink lattes."

Heather looked at them. "I don't know what to do."

"We need to start by calling Cassie. Once we get all the facts, we need to call your mom," Shari said.

"She's right," Madison said. "Your mom is going to have to be here for all the paperwork. She's the only one who can make decisions regarding the business."

"My mom left me in charge," Heather said.

Shari put her arm around Heather. "I understand, but I really think your mom should be here."

"So do I," Madison said. "She will be very angry if we keep her in the dark about this. Knowing your mom, she's checking the sales from a computer in Italy everyday."

Shari nodded her head. "She's right."

"Darling, I have to get going. I have to finish the demo by tonight." Dino gave her a quick peck on the lips. "Shari, would you mind giving her a lift home?"

"Not at all."

Dino pointed at them. "Stay out of trouble. I see the look in both your eyes."

Shari looked at Madison and they giggled.

"Promise," Madison said.

Shari waited for Dino to be out of their sight before speaking. "I need to get in there, look around, see what I feel."

"I knew those were going to be your exact words. I don't think the firemen are going to let us near there while everything is still smoldering," Madison whispered.

"All I need is ten minutes to walk around. I know I'm going to find something. I have a feeling."

Shari rubbed her temples, closing her eyes. *The sound of heels echoed in the street. As the sound got closer, she kept her eyes on the street. They were black boots with a one-inch thick heel. Fringe hung from mid-calf down to the ankle. Whoever wore them had small feet, and walked with a hop, more than likely a woman. She walked along the side of the store before disappearing around the back.*

As the vision ended, Shari's eyes busted wide open. "I'm going in there tonight. I'm not taking no for an answer. I think the answer we are looking for is going to be in the store."

"I don't know, Shari."

"Here comes Aunt Cassie and Sophia." Heather waved.

"Hopefully Cassie comes up with something," Shari said. "She's the professional."

Cassie and Sophia made their rounds hugging and kissing everyone hello. The five of them stood with their arms crossed staring at the gray smoke still escaping out the front windows. Reaching over to Heather, Shari took her hand in hers. One at a time they joined hands, standing in a circle.

"We need to make some decisions," Cassie said letting go of Sophia and Madison's hands. "Why don't we go get a cup of coffee?"

"Sounds like a wonderful idea," Shari said leading the way.

Shari walked to the left side of the diner and slid into the circular booth in the back. Basically they had the whole place to themselves except for the table of six women on the opposite side of the diner.

Claire walked over to them with the pot of coffee. "Are you ladies doing coffee or lattes this morning?"

"Lattes with extra whip cream for all of us," Shari said. "I'll also have a sesame seed bagel with butter. Anyone else?"

Madison licked her lips. "Me too."

"We'll all have bagels. Three with butter, two with cream cheese." Shari picked all the menus off the table handing them to Claire.

"Is there anything I can do to help?" Sophia asked.

"Not at the moment," Shari said. "But I can sure use your help later on."

"I don't like the sound of this," Madison said. "I can tell you are up to no good. You already have a game plan."

"Oh how well you know me." Shari took her iPad out of her handbag. "I think we have procrastinated long enough. I'm going to call Fay."

"You want me to call?" Madison asked.

"No, need to. I have Skype already downloaded." Shari placed her tablet on the table. "We will all tell her."

"Perfect," Sophia said.

Shari punched in the numbers. Within minutes, Fay answered holding a navy blue espresso cup in her hands.

"Good evening," Fay said. "I can't believe you called. I just talked about you to my cousin Maria. I'm going to take you outside to see the gorgeous sunset. How are the girls?"

"We're all here," Madison said.

"Let me see."

Shari lifted her iPad, circling it around the table.

"My baby's there with you too. That's awesome. Thank you for taking care of her. She's the only one I worried about, but from what I see, everyone looks great." Fay pushed her hair behind her ears. "I love it here. I wish you guys could come. I promise you once you step foot on Italian ground, you aren't going to want to go home."

"Is that why you extended your stay for another month?" Cassie asked.

"Or did you meet a pure breed Italian stallion who you can't part with?" Sophia added.

Fay grinned. "How well you ladies all know me? Hey are those lattes I see on the table?"

"Yes," they all said at once.

"I'm enjoying my morning cappuccino and double espresso at night." She giggled. "During the day, I venture out into the bazaars and local shops picking up lots of items for the store. I sent a few boxes to Heather at the house. Wait until you see…"

Shari blocked out the rest. Fay seemed so alive, content. It had been a long time since she sounded this bubbly. Even while married to Angelo, Fay very rarely had the spark in her eyes she had now.

"What's going on with you guys? How's Dino?"

Shari turned her iPad toward Madison. Apparently, Fay had walked outside where the green of the countryside was in the distance.

"He's doing much better, thank God." Madison leaned into the table. "When exactly are you coming home?"

"I'm not sure. Maybe in a couple of weeks."

Madison leaned into Shari and whispered, "We got to tell her."

"Tell me what?" Fay asked, her eyes narrowing.

Shari looked at her friends, who dropped their eyes from her gaze, except for Madison. Madison moved closer to Shari so they were both visible to Fay.

"Something has happened that we all agreed you need to know," Madison said.

"Is Heather okay?"

Heather slipped out of her seat and kneeled on the bench behind Shari and Madison. "Can you see me, Mom?"

"Yes, I can see the three of you. Now are you going to tell me what's going on?"

Shari turned her iPad to her face. "Fay, something devastating happened here. We didn't want to call you, but we all decided you needed to know."

Fay rested her hands under her chin. "You're scaring me."

Madison tilted the tablet toward her. "There was a fire at your store early this morning."

Fay stared at them expressionless, even as tears rolled down her cheeks. "Are you sure?"

"Yes," Shari said.

"Was the fire an accident? I know I should have fixed the light socket in my office."

"I'll get more information for you tomorrow. I don't think it was an accident. I'm under the understanding the fire broke out in the basement. I promise we'll have more answers for you tomorrow."

Fay brought a white laced hankie to her face to wipe the tears away. "I'm coming home."

"It's okay. We can handle everything on our end," Shari said.

"No. Let me see my daughter, Shari."

Shari handed Heather her iPad. By the look on Heather's face, Shari knew at any moment she would break down. Right on cue, Heather began.

"Oh, Mom. Things are terrible here. The store is gone. The side windows are blown out with flames all over the place. The firemen squirted water into the store for over an hour so far," Heather blurted it out without taking a breath. When she finished, she handed Shari back the iPad.

"I see you left out some important things."

"We had all decided to get all the facts first before we called to fill you in," Cassie said. "We still don't have answers, but should have some in a few days."

"Few days, my ass. I'll be home as soon as I can get a flight out. Heather, I will call you for the specifics."

Shari held out her hand. "Give me the iPad." By the time Shari had the iPad in her possession, Fay had disconnected. "She's gone."

"That gives us limited time to figure out what's going on," Cassie said.

"What are we going to do?" Sophia asked playing with the napkin under her latte. "How are we going to get answers?"

"We're going to get answers because I'm going in there," Shari said.

"Oh no." Madison held up her hand. "We were already warned we can't go into the store until there is a full investigation."

"Yeah. Your point?" Shari held up her latte when the waitress passed. "I'll have another one on your way back. Anyone else?"

Madison, Sophia and Cassie all nodded their heads yes. Heather stood, throwing her handbag over her shoulder.

"Where are you going?" Madison asked.

"I'm going home to make some calls. I have to contact the insurance company to get an adjuster down to the store as soon as possible."

"Sit down. We'll do it for you," Madison said.

"That's okay, Aunt Madison. I am very tired. I honestly need to go home, make my phone calls and lie down. I have an unbelievable migraine."

"If you change your mind or need any help, give us a call," Shari said.

"I will." Heather kissed them all. "I'll call you guys later."

Shari waited for her to leave before continuing the conversation. "I need to get into the store. I know the answers we are looking for are in there. I can feel it. I can get into the store from the back."

"I don't know about this," Sophia said. "I think this is dangerous. We should wait until they say we can go in."

"There's no waiting. I need to get in there today. I can feel the vibe."

Cassie broke off a piece of bagel and then popped it in her mouth. "I know I'm going to regret saying this, but I have a plan."

"Now we're talking. Wait," Shari waved her hand when the waitress returned with four lattes. "Since it's too early to drink, we'll have to use our lattes to toast."

"Before we toast, let me tell you my plan," Cassie said.

"We're all ears," Madison said.

"Let's meet back here tonight at nine-fifteen. By then all the shops in the area will be closed except for here. I want you all to come back dressed in black and in sneakers. I also need you to bring flashlights. And most importantly, not a word about what we're doing to anyone."

Shari raised her latte, whispering, "So mote it be."

They all held up their cups in a toast.

"So mote it be."

* * * *

Shari arrived at the diner at nine-twenty. Madison, Cassie and Sophia sat in the booth in the back of the diner drinking coffee. Shari slid in next to Sophia, signaling to the waitress for a cup of coffee.

"What's the game plan?" Shari asked.

The waitress placed a cup of coffee in front of her. "The coffee is on the house. That's the last of the pot. We're closing in ten minutes."

Shari lifted her cup. "Thank you." When the waitress walked back behind the counter, she leaned into the table. "Sorry I was running a few minutes late. Thomas hung onto my leg trying to stop me from leaving."

"Not a problem. I've been meaning to stop by to see him," Cassie said. "I promise to make time to come over during the week."

"Once we get through this, I'm going to set up a dinner party for us. I'm dying to see Antonio and Scott again. You girls hardly bring them around," Shari said sipping her coffee.

"I know," Sophia said. "I'm just so busy with work. I'm lucky if I spend a couple of hours a week with him."

Cassie nodded her head. "Same here. I've been so busy. We're both working totally different shifts. When we do spend time together, well…I don't want to share him if you know what I mean."

"We need to make time to see each other. I can't remember the last time we had our monthly meeting," Madison said. "I miss us all hanging out together."

"It's been tough without Fay. Now with the fire, it's like our world is falling apart," Cassie said. "But we have to stay on top of things. It's up to us to figure out what's going on."

"Let's not do any speculating." Shari stood. "Let's go see what we can find."

"If we don't?" Cassie asked.

"I don't think that's even an option. I know what we're looking for is there," Shari insisted.

They each left a dollar bill on the table for the waitress before walking out of the shop.

Taking gloves and black ski hats from her pocket, Cassie handed each of them a set. "It is extremely important you have these on at all times. Any mistakes could land all of us in jail. Leave behind a strand of hair or one of our fingerprints in the wrong place and we'll be hauled away."

"Not to worry. We are smart. We want to get the bitch that did this. I want to see her behind bars," Madison said, sliding the hat on.

"You guys watch too many cop shows on television. In real life the good guy hardly ever gets rescued," Cassie said.

"Now that's reassuring," Sophia said.

Shari walked ahead of them. She knew they were going to spend the night bickering back and forth, especially Cassie and Sophia. They didn't have much time and she needed complete silence if she were going to find out anything.

Standing outside the backdoor, she closed her eyes. She heard the girls pass by her on the stairs and walk through the backdoor, but she stayed where she felt something.

"Do I want to use the backdoor or the cellar door? Rummaging through her handbag, she took out an ice pick and hammer. As she stepped down the two stairs, the ice pick fell out of her hand. Shit. *Looking around in the dark, she couldn't find where it went. How could she have forgotten to bring a flashlight?"*

Shari reached into her jacket pocket and took out her flashlight. Looking around, she didn't see anything, but then something caught her eye. Walking back up the stairs, she spotted the ice pick covered with debris from the fire. Shari took a piece of hot pink paper out of her back pocket, tore it in fours and crumbled it into a ball. She placed a piece down right next to the ice pick so she didn't forget where she found it.

Continuing down the stairs, she pushed open the backdoor.

"I can't believe I am standing here struggling with the backdoor. My God. That fat bitch must think she has gold in here. All that's here is a bunch of junk, the shit other people don't want. This store just ruins the neighborhood."

While hitting the backdoor with the hammer, she accidentally got her hand in the way smashing her fingers, causing two of her fingernails to break off. "Damn it. I just got a manicure." She kicked the door and it flung open.

Shari looked around the area with her flashlight. She had to find the fingernails but it was just too dark to see anything. Dropping to her knees, Shari picked up a piece of wood to push the debris and ashes around. Somewhere in the basement were the two nails the bitch had lost.

Something told Shari to look to her left. She knew finding anything would be nearly impossible, but she had to appease her curiosity. Slowly, she went through the water and ashes. Then out of the corner of her eye, something shiny caught the light of her flashlight. She spotted a long shiny purple fake nail off in the corner. Again, she took another crumbled piece of hot pink paper out of her pocket and placed it on top of the nail. Another nail lay somewhere in the ashes and soot, but she'd leave it for the investigators to find.

Making her way across the basement, she shook her head in disbelief. The smell of fire was extremely evident. Any merchandise that wasn't in sealed plastic containers, had been totally ruined. Opening the cover on one of the hot pink containers, she shined the flashlight in. The clothes were dry. She signed in relief. Continuing across the basement, she stopped at the bottom of the stairs to the store, where two cans of lighter fluid sat.

Shari could hear the girls talking upstairs. She took the steps two at a time and joined them in the store. Madison, Cassie and Sophia walked around going through the merchandise.

"What are you guys doing?"

"We are waiting for you," Madison said lifting a black and red scarf off the charred display table. "Everything is ruined."

"I don't think if we took any of the clothes home to wash the smell would come out."

"I keep telling you, we can't take anything out of the store," Cassie said. "We aren't even supposed to be in here. Are you almost done?"

"I am done. I found the ice pick, and one of two purple nails she left behind down in the basement."

Cassie's eyes bulged open. "You didn't touch anything, did you?"

Shari shook her head from side to side. "Nope. I did drop a piece of hot pink crumbled paper near the evidence."

"Let's get out of here," Madison said, "before someone catches us."

"I agree." Cassie took her phone out of her pocket. "Give me a few minutes. I'm going to call Antonio, see what he says."

While Cassie called Antonio, Shari walked behind the counter. She opened the cash register, still filled with money.

"Hey, stop playing with everything," Cassie ordered. "I just hung up with Antonio. He said for us to all hightail our asses out of here before we get caught. We are to meet him here tomorrow morning at seven-thirty. I assured him you didn't touch anything."

"I didn't. And besides," Shari took off her gloves, "my hands were protected with latex."

Cassie took her hat off. "Dispose of your things when you get home. Bury them in your garbage. I'll see you in the morning."

Chapter Two

Shari arrived last. On the way, Cassie had texted her asking her to meet them at the back of the store. Shari parked her car around the corner, creeping along the side of the building. She bumped immediately into Cassie.

"You're late," Cassie pointed at her watch.

"Yeah, it's seven thirty-five. What's the big deal?"

"Nothing." Cassie waved her off.

Shari looked around. "Sophia is late too."

"Sophia isn't coming."

"Why?" Shari asked.

"Because this isn't a friendly get-together. Besides, Sophia wasn't involved in any of this originally."

Shari looked at Madison who rolled her eyes and shrugged her shoulders. She had picked up some tension between the cousins without either one saying a word to her. But today, she had to put her suspicions on hold while she dug deep into the situation at hand.

"Here comes Antonio with the inspector guy." Cassie pointed.

"Hey babe." Antonio gave Cassie a quick peck on her lips. "This is Oliver Winters, ladies. And Oliver, this is the Nancy Drew dream team."

They all shook hands before stepping back in place.

"Oliver will be doing the inspection. I filled him in on the way here."

"Thank you, Antonio. I need to ask you ladies if you touched anything when you were in here last night."

"I'll speak for all of us in saying we all wore gloves. I didn't touch anything. I just left crumbled pink paper where I found something," Shari said. "Like right over here." Shari walked over to the pink paper. "Under the paper is the ice pick she lost when she broke into the building."

Oliver adjusted his big wire glasses on his face. "How do you know the ice pick was used to break-in?"

"I just know."

Oliver massaged his chin, then squeezed his lips, looking deep in thought. Shari had a feeling this had been a mistake. How could she explain to this man she saw the break-in in a vision? Shari shuffled from one foot to the other. She didn't need to look up to know everyone's eyes were on her.

"Explanation please," Oliver ordered.

Shari looked up. Cassie and Madison both nodded their heads.

"I had a clairvoyant vision. I'm sure if you ask Antonio," she tilted her head toward him, "he can verify my work with the police department through the years."

Opening the black leather folder, Oliver jotted down a few things on the white legal pad before closing it. "Yes, Antonio has told me about your work. I must admit I am impressed, even though I don't believe in psychic phenomenon. But I am willing to hear your tale."

"I take my work seriously." Shari rested her hands on her hips. "I have helped solve dozens of cases. So if you think I am telling you this because I am in anyway responsible for this fire, then you are talking to the wrong person."

Madison walked next to Shari, resting her hand on her shoulder. "Hey, it's okay. Oliver is just one of those people who don't believe." Madison raised the palm of her hands to face the sky. "Now are you going to give her a chance to tell you what she saw?"

Cassie stepped in the middle of them. "Hey guys, Antonio did us a favor pushing up our inspection. Let's get started. I have an appointment at nine."

"Okay. I'm sorry," Shari said. "Let's begin." Shari walked over to the crushed piece of hot pink paper. "Under the paper is the ice pick. The way I see it is she had a handful of things. The ice pick fell out of her hands."

Oliver slid on a pair of blue gloves and bent down, pushing the paper out of the way. He lifted the ice pick up and placed it into the plastic evidence bag. "Anything else?"

"Yes."

Oliver handed her a pair of blue gloves. "Don't touch anything without the gloves."

"I know. Like I told you, I've been involved in other police investigations."

Oliver didn't seem impressed at all. Instead he seemed annoyed to be there. "Whatever. Now can we continue?"

Shari started down the steps with Madison following. Before Madison hit the bottom step, Oliver lifted his arm stopping both of them.

"Now what?" Shari asked.

"This isn't a party. I want to get in and out of here. I can't have anybody contaminating or disrupting the area until a full investigation takes place. I'm doing this as a favor to Antonio. Therefore, only Shari and I will be going downstairs. Understood?"

"Yes," they all mumbled.

Oliver handed Shari a flashlight. "Now lead the way." He swung his arm toward the stairs.

Shari walked down the four steps, then pushed open the door with her foot. Shining the flashlight in the dark basement, she located the hot pink paper. "Over there, under the paper you will find a purple fingernail. Now I know there's another one down here, but I couldn't find it last night."

Oliver walked through the rubble shining his flashlight on Shari's marker. Squatting down, he lifted the paper, looked at the nail, and then over his shoulder at her. Shari watched him take a tweezers out of his pocket, then lift the purple nail. Opening the evidence bag, he dropped the nail in.

Shari stood in place watching Oliver shine his flashlight on the basement floor. After walking around the area for five minutes, he stopped and squatted down again.

"Well I'll be damned." He turned around to face Shari. "Here's the second nail. This one has some damage to it, but nevertheless I found more evidence."

"I knew it. Hopefully you can pick up some DNA."

Ignoring her, he walked toward the stairs leading to the store. "What else do you have in your bag of tricks?"

Shari walked to the stairs, being careful not to step on anything. "What do you mean?"

"Nothing."

Shari rounded the corner at the top of the stairs, walked into the retail area. Covering her mouth, she gasped. The light of day made the damage look so much worse. Everything Fay had worked hard for had been totally destroyed. Mannequins were broken on the floor. Sweaters and shirts were full of ashes and soot, lying in puddles of water. The oak showcase had some charred damage, but the glass remained intact. Running her covered finger over the wood, she pushed some of the soot and ashes to the side. This piece had been Fay's prized possession. It had been passed down from one generation to the next.

"What's in this room over here?" Oliver asked standing in the archway.

"Fay's office," Shari said walking over to the door. Inside, the office had been riffled through. There were papers all over the floor, which were now covered in water. Apparently, the bitch was looking for something in particular. But what? And how would they prove any of this.

Shari turned to walk out of the office when a chill ran through her. Leaning against the wet table, she closed her eyes.

"Keep looking. I know it's in here somewhere." She began tapping her fingernails against the table when she realized she lost a second nail. *"That's just great. Now I have to go back to the salon. Those little whores swore these nails could withstand any physical activity."*

She tugged on the file cabinet drawers. Maybe she taped the key under the drawer or behind the drawer never expecting anyone to be smart enough to think of looking there. Come on come out, you bastard." This time she tugged so hard the drawer came out of the file cabinet. She emptied it upside down, along with the other four drawers, coming up empty. She couldn't figure out where Fay, the idiot, could have possibly hid the key. *"The hell with it."* Lighting a match, she placed it in the pile of papers on the floor. Hurrying back down the stairs, she squirted the lighter fluid she found earlier all around the basement before dropping another match and escaping out the backdoor.

"The bitch was looking for a key," Shari said.

"What key?" Oliver asked dumbfounded.

"I don't know. She pulled everything apart looking for it. When she couldn't locate the key, she started the fire." Shari pointed to the pile of papers drenched in water in the middle of Fay's office. "The fire started up here. Then on the way out, she squirted the lighter fluid, starting the fire in the basement."

"Now isn't this interesting how you know exactly what happened."

"Please. I told you I have visions. That bitch is the one who started the fires."

"Do you know if Fay had a security system?"

Shari nodded her head. "Yes, but it looks like it was destroyed by the fire."

Oliver walked up and through to what used to be the front door, which more than likely the firemen had busted. Shari followed behind. She met the girls standing outside, along with Antonio.

"How did things go?"

"Everything went fine. Oliver thinks I'm out of my mind."

"So what else is new," Cassie said.

"Ladies, I want you to stay away from this establishment. You are not to go back in there conducting your own investigation. Understood?" he firmly asked.

They all nodded their heads yes.

"I'll see you later." Antonio pressed a kiss on Cassie's forehead before leaving with Oliver.

Shari waited until Antonio and Oliver pulled away in the car before walking back toward the store. Something told her she needed to find the key Benita was searching for.

"Hey," Madison called after her. "Don't play with fire."

Shari turned around with her hands on her hips. "Fay hid a key in there that we need to find. I believe it's what this freak had been looking for."

"I think we should wait until we have full clearance to go in there. And besides, Dino called. He wants me to come home. He said there's a storm approaching the New York City area with heavy rain. They are evacuating parts of Staten Island."

"Yeah, just like they did last year. We all evacuated. As usual, the meteorologist got everyone crazy for nothing," Cassie said. "Besides, look at the sky. It is blue as blue can be. I can't imagine a storm coming through."

"Neither can I. But I don't want Dino to worry. I'll talk to you later." Madison gave the girls a hug before taking off.

"Guess we might as well get going," Shari said. "I promised Thomas I would get him chicken nuggets along with macaroni and cheese."

"Oh to be a kid again." Cassie gave her a hug. "I'm going to stop by the precinct and see what Antonio has to say. We'll touch base later on."

* * * *

Sophia pulled into a parking spot. This morning she had an early appointment, early meaning before noon. These were the appointments she hated. She loved sleeping until ten o'clock. Last night, she stayed up past eleven working, cutting her downtime. Every night she tried to keep the last hour of the day to herself. As she worked on a new centerpiece, she lost track of the time. Thinking about things, she'd bet her business would definitely be a great basis for a television reality show. Why not? These days they created reality shows for everything.

Her job really had no restrictions or time schedule, except on the days parties took place. Her job then required her to stay, sometimes over twelve hours, making sure the parties were running smoothly. Cassie had gotten her this job last year. Thanks to this opportunity, she moved out of her one bedroom apartment and settled into a two bedroom town house in Great Kills.

Sophia loved her job, but hated the coffee. A small price to pay for the big paycheck she received every week regardless if she worked or not.

Outside a few of the kitchen workers stood in a corner talking. As she approached them, they quieted. Was this her imagination playing games with her or were they plotting something?

She had been told through the years, the chefs and kitchen staff constantly changed. Watching them today she had a feeling they were looking for something, be it more money or vacation days. Instead of walking into the lobby, she walked over to the staff.

"Good morning. Please don't stop talking because of me."

"Oh no *señorita*. We don't talk about you," Felipe, the older of the group said. "We," he pointed to the others, "are concerned about the storm that is coming in."

"I think things will be okay. I didn't hear anything about it," Sophia admitted.

"They say big storm coming. Could possibly be a tsunami," Maria said. "I scared. I have two kids, a dog, a deadbeat husband at home. News say evacuation of shoreline. Vincenzo says the storm coming is all nonsense. We can't leave cause of party tonight."

"I promise you guys I will check the weather. As soon as I hear anything, I will come down to the kitchen, let you know. If there is an evacuation, then we all have to leave."

"*Gracias señorita*," Felipe said. "You different than the other people. You care."

"And have gorgeous boyfriend." Maria giggled.

"Thank you, Maria. Now if you have any concerns at all, come up to my office or call me."

Sophia waved goodbye as she walked into the building. What the hell were they talking about? She didn't hear anything at all about a big storm. But then again, the meteorologists always exaggerated, causing extreme mayhem, which would explain why the shelves in the food store were practically empty last night.

Once she got settled in, she turned the television on to channel five. While she waited for the weather to come on, she got all the paperwork ready for her appointment. Sophia was meticulous when booking a party. Her main goal was for the client to feel one hundred percent confident their party would be a huge success without them having to stress over it.

Her appointment this morning was with Clara and Andrew Williams, founders and owners of Children Dreams, non-profit organization. The husband wife team had started the organization five years ago after they lost their son in a hit and run accident. They were prominent people in the community with Andrew Williams running for District Assemblyman in the upcoming election.

As soon as she heard, *hurricane force winds*, she immediately directed her attention to the television. The kitchen staff had been right. The mayor called for an evacuation for everyone who lived on the shoreline. But, then again, last year they said the same thing for Hurricane Irene. Everyone evacuated and the hurricane turned into a tropical storm. The same would be for Hurricane Sandy. *Hell, they lived in New York City.* They never had severe hurricanes.

A knock on her door shifted her attention to her assistant, Dana. "Mr. and Mrs. Williams are here."

"Wonderful. Send them in. Please bring in a carafe of coffee, hot water for tea and put together a small continental tray."

"Gotcha."

Sophia clicked off the television and stood when they walked in, extending her hand out. "Good morning Mr. and Mrs. Williams, welcome to Spotlight."

They both shook her hand. "It's a pleasure to meet you. Please call me Andrew."

"Same here, Clara," she added shaking her hand. "We've spent so much time on the phone. I'm happy to sit here and discuss the endless possibilities for this year's fund-raiser."

Sophia led them to the small round table in the corner by the window overlooking the boardwalk. "Please take a seat while we wait for Dana to return with breakfast. I'll get the books for us to go through."

"Thank you," Clara said sitting.

Dana returned in a flash, placing a small white dish in front of all three of them, along with a cup and saucer. "Coffee or tea?" she asked them.

"We'll both have coffee, thank you," Claire said, helping herself to a bagel. "I've been looking forward to seeing all the things we've discussed the past week."

"I think I've put together a package deal that is exactly what you're looking for within your price range."

"Honestly, money isn't an issue." Clara opened the folder she had brought with her. She took out a piece of paper and slid it across the table. "As you can see, this year, everyone has been so generous. The donations just flooded in without us having to make any calls at all."

"Last year, we had a fund-raiser, small scale at a local restaurant. But as our organization grows, we need more room to accommodate everyone," Andrew explained.

"This will be the first year we would like to go with a DJ for the older kids and parents. We also want to have some activities for the younger kids. Do you have any recommendations?"

"Yes. I can make a few phone calls. I'll put together a proposal for you."

"Excellent," Claire said. "I heard you make awesome centerpieces."

"That I do," Sophia said proudly, handing Claire her portfolio. "Do you have a time frame for when you would like to have this party? If you prefer the warmer weather, I can arrange to have some inflated rides put out on the beach for the younger kids."

"I love the idea," Claire said. "So keeping that in mind, why don't we see if you have a date available on a Saturday afternoon in the summer."

"We're talking an all day party," Andrew said. "The afternoon will revolve around activities for the younger kids and at night for the teenagers. Maybe even a room for the parents."

Sophia opened the appointment book starting at June. "Looks like June is all booked," she said going through each weekend, along with July. Thankfully there was one Saturday open in August. "How does the second week of August sound? That's the first available opening."

"Perfect," Claire said with Andrew agreeing. "Put us in." She took out two checks from the front of her folder. "Here's a five thousand dollar deposit for the hall. And as we discussed on the phone, here's a thousand dollar deposit for the centerpieces and favors." Claire pulled another sheet of paper out of the folder. "This is a breakdown of the boys and girls along with their ages. Please, like I told you, money is no object. We," she pointed to them, "take pride in doing this every year. It's our way of giving back to the community."

"I've put together a whole bunch of ideas. I am really excited about this project."

"So are we," Claire said. "Do you have the paperwork for us to sign?"

"Right here."

"I don't want you to think we're rushing you, but we have to get home, pack a bag and go stay with my mom who lives on higher ground," Claire said. "If you're in the coastal zone, I suggest you take a bag and get to higher land too."

"I just heard about the storm earlier," Sophia said.

The Williams both signed the contract.

"It's really a pleasure finally meeting you." Claire stood. "I look forward to working with you on this project."

"So do I."

* * * *

"Hey beautiful."

Sophia looked up from her desk. Scott stood in her doorway with a dozen red and pink roses.

"What are you doing here, sexy?" she asked standing up, kissing him.

"Surprising you."

Sophia took the roses from him and laid them down on her desk before wrapping her arms around his neck. "The nicest surprise in a long time. How long are you staying?"

"As long as you can put up with me." He wrapped his arms around her waist and squeezed.

"I could never get tired of you."

"Do you really mean that?" he asked stepping back.

"Of course I do. I love you. I hate when you leave."

"Then I have a proposition for you."

Sophia stepped back, crossed her arms and leaned her butt against her desk. Whenever she looked into his blue eyes, she got lost. "Tell me?" she asked pulling him into her arms.

Scott shuffled a few steps back, not making eye contact. But when he spoke again his eyes met hers with a nervous vulnerability. "How would you feel about us living together?"

Sophia's mouth dropped open. This was the last thing she expected him to ask her, but a pleasant surprise. Especially since during the past few weeks, she had many questions in regard to their relationship.

"Well?"

"Yes." Sophia threw her arms around his neck. "I'd really like that."

Scott wiped the back of his hand along his forehead. "Thank God, because I have a car full of things."

"You're kidding me? You were that sure I would say yes."

"Maybe a little hesitant at first, but after talking to you yesterday, I had no doubt you were going to say yes." Scott snickered. "Okay truth be told, I wasn't sure at all if you were going to say yes." Scott extended his hands out to her. "Come here."

Sophia took his hands and twirled around in his arms. "Is this what I can look forward to?"

"Yes. We will dance each night away."

"Knock, knock." Dana stood in the doorway. "I hate to interrupt you lovebirds, but your next appointment just arrived."

"Thank you, Dana. Please offer them a beverage. I'll be with them in a few minutes."

Sophia lifted her key ring off the desk and removed her house key dangling on its own heart chain. "Here you go. Go unpack your car."

"Sounds super. After I unpack, I'm going to take a ride back home, pickup a few more things before I close up my house. Do you need anything from your house while I'm up there?"

"No thanks. I really don't have anything of value up there." *Except for the last box of letters and mementos still sitting on the top shelf of my closet. At least I had the chance to burn the ones describing the dark side of my life.*

"I'll see you in a couple of hours. Where should I leave your key?"

"No need to worry. I have a spare in my wallet."

Scott gave her a hug and a peck on her cheek. "See you tonight."

Chapter Three

On the way home, Madison got a call from Sophia asking her to meet her at the boardwalk, the excitement in Sophia's voice being so evident that without hesitation, Madison agreed. When she called Dino to tell him of her delay, she could hear the disappointment in his voice. She assured him she'd be home within the hour.

The Sand Lane parking lot was packed. Madison drove around the circle finding a spot in The Finn's parking lot, ignoring the sign that read for *The Finn customers only*. She recognized Sophia's car and pulled next to it. As she walked up the ramp, Sophia stood waiting against the railing dressed in a floral sundress and high heels. Hard to believe she could walk in them without the heels getting stuck between the boards.

"Hey Madison," she yelled, her voice echoing causing people to turn around.

Madison waved, letting her know she spotted her. Before walking up the ramp, she glanced at her watch. *Okay, it's twelve-thirty. I have to keep it short, not let her talk me into grabbing a cocktail at The Finn.*

Sophia air kissed her. "Thanks for coming."

"You sounded pretty excited, piquing my curiosity."

"So much has happened in the past half-hour that my head is in a spin." Sophia started walking, only to have her heel get stuck between the boards. "Shit!"

"I told you your heel would eventually get stuck one day. Why don't we either go to your office or sit over there." She pointed at the vacant bench.

"Sounds like a plan."

Madison looked up at the sky. The weather had started to change. The deep blue sky had started to fill with white powder puff clouds. When the sun went behind them, Madison could feel a chill in the air.

"So what's going on?" Madison asked, leaning against the silver metal railing.

"You're never going to believe what happened. I'm so excited I feel as if I'm living in a dream."

Madison crossed her arms, pushing her right leg behind her on the lower railing. "Come tell me."

"Scott showed up here earlier. He wants us to live together," she said her face lighting up.

"Oh my God," Madison hugged her. "This is wonderful news. I am so happy for you. When is this going to happen?"

Sophia jumped up and down. "Today."

"Today? Where is he?" Madison asked looking around.

"As we speak, he's dropping off some of his things at my house." Sophia looked at her cell phone. "By now, he's on his way back to Allentown to pick up some of his other possessions before he closes up his house."

Madison smiled, shaking her head side to side. "I can't tell you how happy I am for you. I really like Scott. He's perfect for you."

"I really love him. But I'm so afraid something is going to go wrong."

"Don't even think like that. You deserve to be happy. You waited a long time to find the love of your life."

"I think you're being dramatic," Sophia said, turning to face the ocean. "Hey take a look out there."

"Where?" Madison turned looking at the ocean.

"The waves. We never get waves here."

Madison looked at the one-foot waves breaking into foam along the water's edge. "That's weird. Hoffman's Island, Coney Island, the tip of Sandy Hook and Swimburne Island surrounds us. We never get waves."

"Could it be this storm they are talking about?"

"What storm?" Madison asked.

"I guess you haven't been watching the news. Even the staff is complaining to me they want to go home. I feel bad, but no way can I let them go. There's a big party going on tonight. I won't be home until after midnight."

"Just be careful later on. I'm going to turn on the news when I get home."

"I don't believe it," a familiar woman's voice said.

Madison turned around. Standing in front of her, stood Brooklyn and Mario. "Oh my God." Madison hugged both of them. "I haven't seen you two in years. You look wonderful," she said to Brooklyn. "Oh before I forget, this is my friend Sophia."

"Hi Sophia," Brooklyn and Mario said at the same time.

"Nice to meet you." Sophia nodded, and then raised her hand. "Not to be rude, but I have to get back to work. I'll call you later," she said to Madison before carefully walking back into the building.

"Looks like married life is treating you good too."

"You two got married?" Madison's thick eyebrows shot up.

"Yes, can you believe it?" Brooklyn wrapped her arm through Mario's. "It's almost two years now. Can you believe I finally took the plunge?"

"I knew you would the day you told me you met Mario. He's such a cutie." Madison looked at Mario who blushed.

"We need to get together soon. I still have the same number," Brooklyn said. "Do you?"

"Yes. Maybe sometime next week. Let me check my schedule. I'll give you a call in a few days to set up a date. I can't wait to catch up."

"Perfect. The guys will get along great. It's all about music and sports."

"Wait till I see Dino. I'm going to tell him the way you ladies talk about us," Mario said.

Brooklyn waved him off. "Yeah you guys are worse than us."

"You're not telling me anything I don't already know." Madison laughed.

"You have time to grab a cocktail at The Finn?" Brooklyn asked.

"I wish I could, but Dino's waiting for me."

"Then go. We'll touch base next week. Hopefully we can set something up for next weekend."

Fifteen minutes later, Madison walked into her house to soft music, with bouquets of roses scattered in vases throughout the living room. She locked the door behind her and headed straight through the kitchen to Dino's office, only to be disappointed not to find him there.

"Dino," she called out walking back into the living room.

"I'm upstairs," Dino called down.

"The living room is gorgeous. Thanks for the flowers."

"You haven't seen anything yet. Come walk over to the stairs."

Madison slid her black jacket off and placed it on the couch along with her handbag before going over to the bottom of the stairs. Dino wasn't standing on the landing, but a trail of red and pink rose petals led the way up. Each step had at least a dozen of them scattered. Holding onto the oak railing, she treaded carefully, listening to the sound of the music getting closer.

"Dino, where are you?"

"Follow the rose petals," his voice echoed from down the hall.

Madison walked along the path into their bedroom. Inside, candlelight illuminated the room. Rose petals were scattered all over the bed. Pivoting on the balls of her feet, she looked around, wondering where Dino had disappeared.

"Dino, where are you?"

"Look on the bed," Dino's voice echoed.

Madison took a quick glance around the room again. *Where the hell is he?* She went to walk out of the room, but decided to see what he had placed on the bed. Under the rose petals laid a white negligee. Taking a hint, Madison remained silent as she changed into the soft lace gown. The thin straps fell off her shoulders while the hem ended just inches above her knee. She turned around. In black silk boxer shorts, Dino stood in the doorway, his hands leaning against the molding.

"You look beautiful, my sweet angel."

Madison twirled around as Dino approached her. She ran her fingers from her breasts down to her thighs. "I love it. I love everything. When did you find the time? Didn't you need to get a promo CD done by the end of the day?"

"Yes I did. I finished last night. When you left this morning, I concentrated on doing something special for you, for me…us."

"What's the occasion?"

"There is no occasion." Dino reached out and took her into his arms. "Can't I do something special for the love of my life?"

"Yes. These are the things I love most about you."

"We are in this for the long haul. Nothing will ever tear us apart."

Madison trailed her fingertips along his cheeks. "Loving you has been the only thing in my life I am sure of. With you by my side, I feel secure, fearless. My love for you is so pure."

"That's why I chose white."

Dino wrapped his arms around her waist, crushing her body against his. To her surprise, she could feel his hardness against her belly sending a chill throughout her. She wanted her husband in the worst way. The last time they made love had been before his heart attack.

"You will always be my one and only. I'm here with you forever, no matter what happens. With you, my life is complete." Standing on her tippy toes, Madison kissed his lips.

"You're all mine." He leaned down to scoop Madison into his arms. "I am going to make love to you as many times as I possibly can. Just you and me." He placed her down in the middle of the bed. "There will be no distractions today. No access to the outside world. No television, cell phones or computers. Just like old times, it will be just the two of us."

"When did you turn into such a romantic?"

"The day you walked back into my life."

Dino stepped out of his silk boxers. He ran his hands from her feet up to her thighs, pushing the soft lace over her hips. His lips followed the negligee over her stomach as he gently pushed the lace up over her head.

The warmness of his lips exploring her body drove her crazy. Throwing her head back, he sprinkled soft kisses down her neck, along her breasts. She moaned with pleasure until he slid inside her, causing her to scream in ecstasy. His penetration brought her to not only one, but multiple orgasms, sending a tranquil feeling throughout her afterward. And when he exploded, she could feel him throbbing inside her.

She held onto him tightly, for dear life. What she felt inside, she wanted to feel forever. Their lovemaking had been pure, not blue pill enhanced. It wasn't an easy feat for Dino to keep his erection, but through their love for one another, they took their time, which led to them making love for a second time.

Dino stood, extending his hand out to her. Madison dropped her hand in his as she slid off the bed. He held her in his arms as they danced to love songs. Madison couldn't believe he had put together a CD with all of her favorite love songs spanning back to the sixties.

After they made love and took a brief nap, Dino suggested they go down to the living room where he had another surprise for her. He had taken out the old disco ball and secured it on top of the ladder. One of her favorite songs by It's Not Over blared through the stereo speakers.

Believe me, if you love me

I'll show you everything will be all right

Believe me girl, I'll hold you tight

Dino dipped her at the end of the song. When he took her back in his arms she rested her head on his shoulder.

"I love this. I can dance the night away with you." Madison kissed his neck.

"That's exactly what I have planned. But first, we need to refuel. I bought us skirt steaks with a whole bunch of trimmings."

"Looks like tonight is going to be the perfect night."

* * * *

"Here you go." Shari handed Thomas the small bag full of mini donuts as she unhooked the booster seat.

"Thanks, Mommy."

Shari helped him out of the car. When she turned to face her house, she saw Tommy up on the ladder hammering sheets of plywood over the glass windows of the beauty salon.

"Hey sexy, what are you doing?" Shari asked standing next to the ladder looking up at him.

"I'm protecting your windows."

Looking around, she asked, "From what?"

"The storm. Look at those clouds coming in." He pointed down the block.

"What storm? All I see are a few clouds lurking in the sky."

"Sweetheart, they are doing mandatory evacuations in areas throughout the five boroughs. Everyone living in zones A, B and C are being evacuated."

"Is that us?" Shari asked holding the ladder while Tommy climbed down.

"No. Luckily we don't fit into any of those zones. But according to the meteorologist, we are supposed to be getting seventy mile per hour winds. Possibly even higher."

Shari looked over her shoulder at Thomas sitting on Tommy's closed toolbox eating his donuts getting powdered sugar all over his mouth.

"Do you think the winds are going to break the windows?"

"Yes. Look over here."

Shari followed Tommy to the other window and tapped lightly on the glass. "Keep your eye on the wooden frame."

"What am I looking for?"

"Just watch."

As Tommy tapped on the window, Shari saw the wood starting to slightly move. "Wow. I have to get that fixed."

"I will reinforce the wood tomorrow. Under the tarp," he pointed into the back of his truck, "I picked up a couple of pieces of wood."

"You're the best."

He came down the ladder and kissed the top of her head. "Why don't you go in, start taping the windows making big X's. I left the blue tape on the kitchen table. That would be a huge help."

"I'll take Thomas in with me so you can get done faster."

"Thanks, sweetheart. I'll be done soon. And on the stove, I bought a rotisserie chicken, and some trimmings from the pork store. Maybe you can heat up the sourdough bread too."

"Yummy. You know how to win a gal's heart."

"And, chocolate chip ice cream for Thomas."

"You're spoiling him."

"So do you. That's why there are chocolate covered strawberries waiting for us when Thomas goes to sleep."

"Can't wait." She squeezed his butt. "I have plenty of plans for you later on."

"Here too. Do me one more favor. Make sure you place candles throughout the house. I left a bag with a couple of flashlights by the backdoor."

"You're really taking this storm seriously."

"Yes I am. Go put the news on. I'll be in shortly." He winked.

"Come on, Thomas. Let's go in, see what Daddy's talking about."

"Can't I stay and watch Daddy?" He pouted.

"No," Shari sang shaking her head side to side. "Daddy's doing work. Besides, it's starting to get chilly out here. When we go in, I'll make you hot chocolate with the little marshmallows. Okay?"

"Okay, Mommy." Thomas stood and walked into the beauty salon.

"Lock up the door," Tommy called out. "I'm going to board up the glass door too."

Shari blew him a kiss as she followed Thomas up the spiral staircase after locking the door into the small hallway outside the kitchen. Thomas already sat at the kitchen table with his bag of mini donuts. Thanks to the microwave, Shari had his hot chocolate with marshmallows ready in less than a minute.

"Here you go." Shari kissed the top of his head. "I'll be in the living room. Remember take small sips."

"I know, Mommy. I can burn my tongue."

Shari took the remote control off the cocktail table and turned the television on. Nothing out of the ordinary was on, seemed to be regular afternoon programs. She'd wait for the five o'clock news to get the local forecast.

In the hallway closet, she took out the wicker basket full of candles. The ones in jars she placed on the cocktail and end tables. She made her way upstairs to place candles in her bedroom before continuing upstairs to her mystical room. If for some reason they lost electricity, then she'd have Thomas come stay with them.

When she came back down, she peeked into the kitchen where Thomas still sat at the kitchen table with his hot chocolate and bucket of dinosaurs. He had them lined up on the table quietly playing. *Perfect. This will give me a few minutes to call Madison.* Just as she picked up her cell phone, a special report logo replaced the afternoon talk show.

"This is a special report. The storm is moving up the coast, leaving behind destruction. In some areas the wind is over eighty miles an hour. Mandatory evacuations for zones A, B, and C are being enforced. The storm is expected to hit the New York City area around eight o'clock. Because of the expected high winds, there could possibly be downed lines. Make certain you have candles and flashlights in the event you lose service…"

Shari walked into the kitchen to check on Thomas again before calling Madison. He sat at the table with all the flashlights lit. "Oh no. You have to shut them off. We need these in case of an emergency." She took the flashlights one at a time and turned them off before placing them in the canvas bag except for one she left on top of the refrigerator.

"Can I trust you for two minutes while I run two of the flashlights downstairs to Mom's shop?"

"Promise, Mommy," he said hugging her leg.

Quickly, she dropped the flashlights off on one of the shop's counters. She came back up, making sure she left a flashlight in all the rooms plus two in their bedroom. Back in the living room, Tommy sat on the couch untying his work boots.

"All done?"

"Yes, just in a nick of time. Let me tell you, the winds are really starting to pick up."

"I heard about the storm on the news. You were right. A monster of a storm is on its way. I think we should start a fire." She placed his boots in the plastic tray by the door.

"Want to grab me a beer, babe, while I start a fire?"

"Be right there." Shari walked over to Thomas and kissed his head. "You want to watch television in the living room with me and Daddy?"

"Can I take my dinosaurs?"

"You bet."

Thomas put his dinosaurs into the blue plastic bucket and carried them into the living room. Shari couldn't help but laugh. The plastic bucket was almost as big as him. She placed his empty cup in the sink, grabbed two beers out of the refrigerator and joined her boys in the living room.

Shari handed Tommy his beer before sitting on the couch while watching Thomas who sat on the floor lining up his dinosaurs on the cocktail table. Glancing over to Tommy, she couldn't help but admire his broad shoulders and slight potbelly. Every time she looked at him, she felt the same desire as she did the day he stood in her doorway with his hands leaning on the upper molding of the doorway.

She never expected to fall in love. She needed a plumber. After making close to two dozen phone calls, she came upon Tommy who quoted her the cheapest price. She hired him on the spot. *What the hell.* Just as long as he was licensed, that worked for her.

He did spectacular work. In the beginning he addressed her as Ms. Stafford, until Shari insisted he call her by her first name. At the time, Tommy worked on his own taking on one job at a time. Somewhere between replacing all her pipes and tiling her bathroom, they fell in love. After the first kiss, there was no turning back. They immediately became a couple.

Five years later, her love for him only got stronger. She couldn't imagine living a day without him or Thomas. When she found herself pregnant she didn't know if she should laugh or cry. She did both. Her life had become complete.

"Earth to Shari." Tommy shook her. "That will come later."

"What will come later?" she asked confused.

"Oh." Tommy scooted next to her, putting his arm around her shoulder. "I thought you were reading my mind full of the wild thoughts of what I plan for us later on."

"I wish."

"You looked so intense." He squeezed her shoulder.

"My mind wandered back to the first time we met. When I fell in love with you."

Tommy snickered. "For me, it was the day you bought me a cinnamon raisin bagel with cream cheese and peach jelly. I couldn't believe you knew what I liked. Well...that was before I knew about your gift."

"For me, the day you stood in your black wife beater T-shirt leaning in my doorway. Right then, I knew I found true love."

"Daddy will you play dinosaurs with me?"

"Only if I can be the stegosaurus."

Shari stood. "While you guys play, I'm going to get dinner ready. I also want to give Madison a quick call."

Chapter Four

Sophia tapped her pen on the desk. The sound of the wind howled from outside. By six o'clock everyone should start coming in for the Chinese auction. Walking down to the hall, she went table to table making sure the centerpieces were perfectly placed in the middle. The past week she had worked diligently on these centerpieces. Her favorite was the coffee, tea and chocolate one she made on a pedestal cake plate. She had decorated the outside of the glass cover with beads. On first glance you would mistake them for gumdrops.

Under each centerpiece she had placed a raffle ticket. Each place setting had a raffle ticket in the small butter dish on top of the navy blue and white square dinner plate. Creating this system would eliminate the arguments that happened all the time over who took home the unique creation sitting in the center of the table.

Upon returning to her office, Earl, the owner, sat at her desk looking through her portfolio.

Sophia stood in the doorway with her arms crossed under her breasts. "Hey Earl."

"Sophia. I've been waiting for you." He pointed to her portfolio. "You have some collection here."

"Thank you. I take a picture of everything I make. Some clients want something original, but the majority pick out something from the book."

"You are getting quite the reputation. Since you came aboard, I've been filling my calendar with more PTA and Chinese auction events during the week." Earl closed her portfolio and stood. "Your hard work has not gone unnoticed. You'll have a nice bonus in your next paycheck."

"Thank you, Earl. I appreciate it."

"Oh, before I forget, I cancelled tonight's party, rescheduling it for tomorrow night. Mrs. Lombardi is afraid the weather is going to scare everyone away. I tend to agree. So whenever you're done here, lock up, go home."

"Thank you. Did you tell the kitchen staff?"

"Yes, I did. They will leave when everything is in order." Earl walked to the door. "I'm heading out. My wife is bitching and moaning about the storm. Everyone is getting all crazy over nothing. The meteorologists pulled the same shit last year."

"Then go. I'll go check up on the staff downstairs. Then I have some work to take care of before I leave."

"Catch you in the morning."

Sophia walked around her desk and placed her portfolio back on her credenza. Before she did any work, she would go downstairs to tell the kitchen staff to go home. Earlier, they were really upset about having to stay because of the oncoming storm. She took the backstairs to the kitchen. When she walked into the room, everyone stopped what they were doing to look at her.

"Hey guys," she addressed both the men and the ladies, "why don't you just leave everything, go home to your families."

"We can't," Pedro said. "Mr. Riverman said the kitchen must be spotless before we could go home."

Sophia leaned against the long metal countertop. "I know what he said, but I think if you all come in an hour earlier than your shift, you will be able to wrap things up down here."

"I think Mr. Riverman would be pissed off," Clara said in a heavy Spanish accent.

"I take full responsibility." Looking around, she added, "There isn't much out of place here."

"Are you sure?" a voice from the other side of the kitchen called out.

"Yes. I want all of you to go home to your families."

"Thank you, *señorita*," Pedro said.

Most of the workers personally thanked Sophia on the way out. Once everyone left, she shut the lights off and locked the backdoor. There really wasn't much to do for tomorrow except emptying out the large pots of water. On the way back to her office, she walked out to the cocktail reception room, which led to the boardwalk. Sophia could hear the wind as it shook the room. Opening the door turned into a challenge, with the wind blowing off the ocean.

"Lady, be careful," said a man in a green windbreaker with Parks Department on the back. "Go home. The tide is picking up. You shouldn't be here. Everyone is being evacuated."

"Thanks for the warning," Sophia yelled through the wind. "I'll be certain to be careful."

Ignoring his warning, Sophia walked onto the boardwalk, zippering her jacket and leaned against the wet silver railing, watching the waves break halfway up the beach. She couldn't remember the last time she'd seen the water so high up on the sand. The more the wind picked up, the farther up the beach the waves broke.

Farther down on the boardwalk, going toward the Verrazano Bridge, she spotted a photographer with a large telephoto lens. Crossing her arms, she walked closer to the photographer, who had his camera lens covered in a yellow plastic bag. He looked funny, but smart protecting his gear.

Sophia walked back toward the door to the hall, surprised that supposedly despite all the evacuation warnings, there were quite a few people on the boardwalk just strolling along watching the high tide. This would be the time for her to catch up on all the paperwork she hadn't been able to do the past few weeks. She also had four other parties who wanted specialized centerpieces. One group wanted a sports theme, another a sweet sixteen, with the other two having picked centerpieces from the portfolio. Tonight would be a good night to start putting things together.

Locking and bolting the door behind her, she walked through the building making sure all the staff had left. Pedro, the only one left, continued to work in the kitchen.

"Pedro, what are you doing?" she asked, lifting a dish towel and starting to dry the pots on the metal counter.

"I can't leave without knowing everything is done. I'm the senior member of the staff. Everyone reports to me. This is the right thing to do. I don't want to see you taking responsibility for things being a mess in the kitchen in the morning."

"I appreciate your loyalty, but you have a family at home. Go home," she ordered. "I will finish drying the pots and put them away."

"I don't—"

"Goodbye Pedro. I will see you in the morning. I have to stay here anyway to catch up on work. There is no reason why you have to stay here too."

"Thank you, *señorita*. I will see you tomorrow morning."

"We don't have a party until five. No reason for you to come in before twelve."

"Thank you." Pedro pulled his sweat shirt over his head. "Have a good night."

Sophia placed the last pot in the cabinet before returning to her office. Sitting back in her chair, she took a deep breath. The sound of the wind seemed to be louder. In a strange way the sound of the wind and the ocean roaring was soothing to her ears. The moment she opened her appointment book, her office phone began ringing.

"Good afternoon, Spotlight Caterers. How may I help you?"

"I'm interested in finding a hot sexy woman to bring home with me," Scott said.

"Hey baby. I'm surprised you didn't call my cell phone."

"I did. It went right to voice mail."

Sophia picked up her phone. The words, *no service*, appeared on the screen. "Figures. It's really windy here."

"Sun's shining here. I just finished packing my car. All I have to do is close up the house. Then I'm going to stop by the diner to see my aunts."

"Please send them my love."

"I will. What I'll do is call you when I'm on my way. What time is it?"

"Ten to six."

"I'll see you around nine, nine-thirty."

"Okay. That works out fine. I'll leave here around eight o'clock."

"I put a tray of lasagna and meatballs in the refrigerator my aunts made."

"Yummy. Tell them thank you," she said while doodling on a piece of paper.

"I also have a bottle of champagne chilling."

"You thought of everything."

"Yes I did. Let me get going."

"Okay. Be careful."

"Love you."

She blew him a kiss over the phone. "Love you too."

* * * *

Cassie arrived at Antonio's office early. She waited at his desk while he ran out to pick up their dinner. For some unknown reason, the takeout wait took over an hour and a half. Tonight he had the four to midnight shift at the precinct. Cassie had agreed to take a look at some of the cold cases to see if she wanted to take any on with Shari.

Tonight, seemed really weird. Usually whenever she came to visit Antonio, the phones were ringing off the hook, but for the past twenty minutes the only sound came from the wind blowing outside.

Out of the four-dozen files she went through, she found an interest in two of them. The most important thing to look for was pieces of personal items that Shari could touch, hopefully get some kind of a reading from. One of the cases she picked involved a missing thirty-four year old who by now would be forty-five. The other had been a murder case.

Cassie's ongoing search to find Benita had come to a dead end. She had a strong feeling the woman had returned to the Dominican Republic after being released from jail. Shari disagreed with her. She believed Benita had gotten herself a job working as a real estate agent, living in vacant apartments and houses. Wherever she was hiding, Cassie was happy she had disappeared and stopped harassing her and her friends. On their agenda for Monday morning was to call all the real estate agencies asking for her. Shari had seen her at an apartment on Robinson Place. Calling any agency with the street name might zero into the agency the building is listed with.

Cassie stood, and placed the two folders in her briefcase. On the bookshelf behind his desk, she spotted a couple of pictures of kids. On further inspection, she recognized them as Antonio's two teenage children. The assortment of picture frames ranged from little league baseball pictures to dance recitals, up to the present. Another picture looked like a recent picture of him with both his kids. Cassie smiled. The kids had been rough on her in the beginning, but eventually they warmed up to her. Antonio wanted to take the kids to Florida during spring break and had asked her to join him. She didn't hesitate accepting his invitation.

She had met Antonio during a routine process serving. While she waited for him, she read through the paper work. His ex-wife made him sound like an animal, saying he was abusive to her and the kids. At his court hearing, the judge didn't renew the temporary order. Antonio paid her more child support than required, along with all the kids' activities.

To think she'd almost let him go. To this day she believed he had tested her to see how far he could push her. When he demanded she get him breakfast and have sex, she threw him out of her house. But her brother Bruce saw something different reuniting them at Thanksgiving dinner. Since then, Antonio had done everything in his power to make things right, perfect. He had succeeded in winning her heart.

A loud scream coming from outside, pulled Cassie's attention to the window. As she stood, she saw the long glass window shake on the opposite side of the thick silver rusted gates. Looking out, she watched people running in all different directions. Leaning against the gate, she watched the street fill with water as waves broke over the concrete wall. She couldn't believe her eyes. This wasn't the ocean, but a wide canal used for cargo ships coming from Manhattan harbor, passing under the Verrazano Bridge, out into the Atlantic Ocean. The image of water flowing down Richmond Terrace scared her. People had abandoned their car in the middle of the street, as the streets became desolate.

Cassie turned around. Standing at the door were two plainclothes officers with a grin on their faces.

"Can I help you two guys?"

The younger, shorter of the two took a step back. "No."

"Just checking out Antonio's taste," said the other officer.

Cassie nodded her head and grinned. Apparently Antonio had been bragging about her to a

few of his colleagues.

"Whatever you're doing, keep doing it. He's been bearable to work with." He offered her his hand. "I'm Joel Avers. This is my partner Jimmy Landers."

Cassie shook their hands. "It's a pleasure to meet the two of you."

"I don't know how Antonio always gets so lucky," Jimmy said. "Every woman I meet turns into a nightmare."

"That's why you have to take the leap. Find yourself a bride, settle down."

"In your dreams." Jimmy laughed. "I very much enjoy being a bachelor."

"Let's go, casanova. This storm is coming in. I'm sure people will be acting like complete idiots," Joel said, walking toward the door. "Nice to meet you. Tell Antonio he is one lucky guy."

"I will."

Their sneakers squeaked down the high glossed waxed hallway. Cassie could hear them talking about Antonio. A door opened, slammed shut, then silence again. She wondered what was taking Antonio so long. Returning back to the window, she leaned on the gates. Richmond Terrace not only turned into a ghost town, but now looked like a river.

Glancing at her watch, she couldn't believe it had been close to forty-five minutes since Antonio had left. She decided she would go downstairs to see if he was in the building. He more than likely got caught up with something. It wasn't like him to not call her if he got stuck.

"Hey sexy. Miss me?"

Cassie turned around. Soaked from head to toe, Antonio stood at the door with a shopping bag.

"What the hell happened to you?" Cassie asked, walking over to him and taking the wet bag out of his hand. "I was just about ready to come looking for you."

"You wouldn't believe what it's like outside. It's pouring. The water is flowing over the sea wall. I have never seen anything like this before."

Cassie placed the bag on his desk and walked over to the window. "I can't believe Richmond Terrace is a river."

"Baby, this isn't good. You are stuck here with me."

"Hmm, might not be such a bad thing."

"No it isn't, but it's going to be a long night."

"Not a problem." Cassie walked back to Antonio's desk and started taking the contents out of the bag. "I'll head on out after we eat."

"That's the point. The streets are all flooded down here. There is no way you are going to leave here. The water is up to my calves."

"Are you kidding me?"

"No."

"I think it's going to pass over." Sitting, Cassie took the plastic top off her sandwich.

Antonio shook his head. "I don't think so. The wind is picking up. While I waited for our order, the news was on. The mayor spoke, asking people in the evacuation sections to go to high ground. And those who were in high ground to stay in."

"Wow. This must be serious. I wonder if my dad knows." Fumbling through her handbag, she pulled out her cell phone. "Would you mind if I called my dad real quick?"

"Go ahead," he said making room on his desk to place their food.

Cassie dialed her dad's number, to no avail. All circuits were busy. "Would you mind if I use the office phone?"

"No. Go ahead. Looks like the storm has affected the cell phone towers. I had a hard time calling the kids earlier," Antonio said, sitting down.

The phone rang several times before Harry picked up. "Dad, are you okay?"

"I'm fine. I have people waiting for rooms, which aren't available. Seems like the storm has dislocated a lot of residents."

"What are you going to do? And where is Bruce?"

"Bruce is downstairs in the lobby trying to keep the people under control. Everyone is panicking. There just aren't anymore rooms."

Cassie detected fear in her dad's voice. "Dad, I have no access to a television. What's going on?"

"Oh baby, the eye of the storm is going to hit at any given time. The streets are flooded and have downed trees and phone lines all over the island. Most of the roads by the shorelines are sunk. Thank God I'm in the center of the island out of the flood zones."

"I wish I could be there to help you," Cassie said helping Antonio take the condiments out of the shopping bag.

"Stay where you are. I'll be okay."

"I can't go anywhere. Richmond Terrace is washed out. I'm here with Antonio in his office."

"Good. At least I know you are safe. I have to run. I have the kitchen staff putting together platters so I can offer these people something to eat. Hopefully the storm will pass over and everyone will return to their homes in a couple of hours."

"From your lips to God's ears," Cassie said, remembering these were her mom's famous words.

"Love you, sweetheart. Be safe."

"You too, Dad."

Cassie placed the phone back in the cradle. Something wasn't right. She could feel it in her bones. Before sitting down, she walked back to the window. Water was flowing two feet high over the sea wall. The squad cars parked in front of the precinct sat submerged up to their windows. The banners on the flagpoles from the stadium across the street were blowing wildly, with two of the six ripped.

"Antonio, come look at this," she said, over her shoulder. "I can't believe what I'm seeing."

Antonio rested his arm on her shoulder. Silence filled the room. Cassie gazed at him as he looked out the window with fear in his eyes. Maybe she was misreading him, but the way his fingers held on to her shoulder and the quick breaths he took, led her to believe he too knew they were prisoners at the station.

"I'm having a feeling this is going to be a long night," Cassie said taking his free hand in hers. "I'm so glad we're together."

* * * *

Sophia cleaned up her desk. The past hour she did more work than she had done all week. In her office closet, she finally had time to straighten up the bins filled with her centerpiece supplies. This time, she hand wrote a list of everything in the bins, before proceeding to make a spreadsheet. She always seemed to buy the same supplies multiple times.

From what she had seen, all she needed to buy were small and large organza bags. Her clients all loved the small goody bags she made. She sat down behind her laptop. Just as she started to place her order, she heard a loud crash followed by the sound of glass breaking. A chill rushed through her. She flew out of her seat, opened her door and walked down the hallway. The howling wind came from the room overlooking the ocean. Noticing her feet were wet, she stopped dead in her tracks. Looking behind her, the floor remained dry. Could it be someone overflowed the toilet in the main lobby? Yuck.

Continuing down the hall, she heard another crash along with more shattering of glass. For certain, something wasn't right. The closer she got to the room, the higher the water rose on her calves. She unbolted the two wooden doors. The moment she turned the handle and opened the door, water hurried at her.

Sophia held onto the door handle tightly as the entire lobby was engulfed. When the surge started to recede, she stepped cautiously into the hall. To her left, the glass French doors leading to the boardwalk were floating toward the entrance door.

When the wind slowed down, she stared out the doorway. The waves were breaking feet away from the boardwalk, pushing the sand up onto the wooden walkway and into the hall. Pieces of wood and garbage floated past with some pieces drifting into the hall. As the wind began to pick up again, so did the tide, which started to break again even closer to the boardwalk.

In the distance, she spotted a person in a bright orange jacket trudging toward her, waving. Sophia returned the gesture as she watched him fight the wind and rain. By now she had become completely wet. Licking her lips, it wasn't rainwater on her tongue, but ocean water. The taste of salt evident.

"Lady, get out of here," screamed the man as he approached her. "Go home while you can. The ocean is getting fierce. The streets are filling up with water."

"I can't. The doors are gone. Anyone could come in," Sophia yelled above the howling wind.

"Look at the sky, lady. Those are funnel clouds. Get out of here. I'm heading home to my family."

Sophia pushed her wet hair behind her ears. "Okay. I will go. Come with me. We will go out the front doors."

The short stocky man followed her through the catering hall. Sophia heard him yelling something else, but couldn't understand his words. As she walked through the opening into the lobby, something hit her from behind sending her across the room. *Oh my God. What the hell is happening?*

Chapter Five

Boy, did it get cold in here. Brr. Leaning forward, Madison grabbed the quilt at her feet to cover both her and Dino. Being cold was a small price to pay, especially after the afternoon they had together. Turning on her side, she slid her arm around his chest. The bond they had formed the past few months had been incredible. Dino had tried so hard to satisfy her, but today, making love came naturally. They had made love twice that afternoon. He had been unsuccessful the third time around.

Everything had been perfect earlier. Madison longed to feel Dino deep inside her. She wouldn't admit her feelings to him because their relationship consisted of more than just making love. To her, foreplay was where all the love and emotions came from. The sex just complimented the foreplay. Being here with him now, meant everything to her.

All of a sudden, the bedroom got colder causing her to shiver. Once she warmed up, she'd go downstairs to add some wood to the fireplace. As the wind howled loudly on the other side of her locked windows, her curtains moved.

Tomorrow she would look into getting replacement windows in their house, something they had wanted to do for a long time.

Leaning into Dino, she started sprinkling kisses down his neck, shoulder and arms until he rolled around into her arms to face her.

"Hey, beautiful." He pushed her hair out of her face. "How are you feeling?"

"Words can't describe what I'm feeling inside. I love you so much."

"I love you too." Dino kissed her forehead. "I'm hoping earlier broke my dry spell."

"I wouldn't have called it a dry spell. During the past few months we have become closer. We talked more, built a magazine together. You're doing what you love and I'm back to writing again."

"You're right."

Madison leaned on her elbow to face him. "I think it's time to start getting freelance writers and photographers to help with the magazine. We need to lighten our load so we can spend more time like this together."

"I agree. But you have to promise me you'll think about reigniting your book career."

"I don't know if I want to write novels anymore. You can't go back in time."

"Look at us. We went back in time and took things forward. So yes, sometimes you get a chance to go back in time to do things right."

Dino pushed her on her back, sliding on top of her. Pushing her hair off her face, he lowered his lips to hers. Madison closed her eyes as she felt electricity travel through her. Taking her hands, he held them above her head. "We are going to spend the rest of the day in bed. We'll eat hero sandwiches now, and just maybe," he kissed her neck, "you'll let me have a beer while I barbeque the skirt steaks later."

"Maybe one. If you're a good boy." Smirking, Madison trailed her fingers down his cheeks. He'd already been a damn good boy. "Okay, I give up. You can have just one."

"And if I satisfy you all night long?"

"Then breakfast is on me."

Dino released her hands. "You have been so patient with me."

"There's nothing to be patient about. I love you. That's what matters." Madison sat up. "I love the nights we sat in each other's arms watching television. Even better are the nights we laid here in bed cuddling."

"I guess it's just a man thing. I felt I wasn't giving you what you needed. I spent so many nights praying you wouldn't stray."

"Stray? Oh my God, what would ever make you think I would do something like that? I am totally satisfied having you alive, by my side. We're a team."

Dino ran the back of his fingers along her face. "Darling, you can't understand the frustration I felt the past few months. I didn't feel like a man. And besides, you are a beautiful woman. I see how men look at you."

"I'm glad you see, because I don't have a clue. When we reunited, I promised you it would be you and me for the rest of our lives. I meant every word I said. Nothing will ever come between us again." Madison kissed his lips. "Our magazine is a hit. I can't believe the amount of requests in our inbox for bands who want us to interview them."

"I know. I finally have everything. I have the career I always wanted, and I'm with the love of my life."

"I feel the same way." Madison glanced over her shoulder toward the window when she heard a strange noise. "What the hell is that?"

"The wind. Somewhere out there I heard we were going to have high winds."

"That's news to me. But," Madison threw her leg over his, "I can think of something to do instead of going downstairs to play around with the campfire you started earlier."

"I say screw the campfire. I think between the two of us we can heat up the room."

"I couldn't agree more. Are you up to another round?"

Dino lifted the blanket, and looked down. "Honestly, I think junior is exhausted."

Madison giggled. "Yeah, I think you're right. Besides, you have to take it easy. You just got over having open-heart surgery."

"As usual, you're right." Dino sat up. "I'll go down, make us lattes and turn the heat up."

"No. I want you to rest. Once you're a hundred percent recovered, you can return the favor by taking care of me."

"That's a deal."

Madison slipped off the bed, pulling Dino's shirt over her head. *Brrr.* The cold went right through her. She blew out the candle on her nightstand and flicked on the light switch. When the light didn't go on, she looked behind the nightstand checking to make sure the plug still remained in the wall.

Walking to Dino's side of the bed, she clicked on the light switch. Nothing. "Boy, is this strange. Both light bulbs blew."

"Baby, the room was on fire all afternoon. What do you expect," he said, pulling her back onto the bed.

"No, seriously." Madison stood. "Let me try the other light switch. It is highly unlikely both bulbs blew out at the same time." She walked by candlelight to the door. "Let me go get us a drink. I'll grab two light bulbs from the kitchen cabinet."

"Maybe you can grab the two hero sandwiches I bought earlier. I can go for something to eat. And just maybe, you'll be a good girl and bring me up the light beer you promised me."

"I'll think about it," she said over her shoulder.

Madison would give in to Dino's request. One beer wasn't going to hurt him. He had spent the whole day satisfying her, putting his needs second to hers. She had her husband back. Holding onto the oak banister, which became a habit after she had fallen down the stairs, she began walking barefoot down. One step, two steps, three steps, four steps, five steps and then her foot landed in ice-cold water. She let out a scream and ran back up the stairs.

"Oh my God," Madison kept repeating over and over again. By the time she got up the steps Dino stood in the bedroom doorway.

"What's wrong?"

"Water." Madison pointed to her feet. "I stepped in water."

"What are you talking about?"

"I walked down the stairs. There's water. I couldn't see much but it looked high. Oh dear, oh God." Madison felt her body tremble. "Something's wrong," she cried. "I think the first floor is filled with water."

Dino opened his nightstand drawer and pulled out a mega flashlight. "I have the big gun." He laughed.

"Dino, I feel it. Something's wrong."

Dino extended his hand to her. "Come on. I'm going to prove your mind is playing games with you."

"I swear. I touched water on the sixth step. I'm not lying."

Madison walked closely behind Dino who continued to chuckle. She hated when he did that. That chuckle meant he thought she was exaggerating. Dino waved the flashlight at the light switch. He flicked it up, nothing.

"Shit." He turned around flashing the light in her face. "I think it's safe to say we have a blackout, which I can't say I'm surprised with the wind. Damn," he pointed up, "the wind is still gusting."

They walked down the hall to the steps with Dino leading the way. He stopped at the top. "Holy shit."

"What?" Madison walked next to him, looking down the stairs. There were no stairs except for the top two steps. The rest had been filled with water. "Dear God. I told you Dino. And I swear, I counted six steps before I stepped into water."

"Something is not right. What's going on?"

"I have no idea, Dino," she said in a panic. "What are we going to do?"

Dino turned to face her. "The first thing we need to do is stay calm. Let's go back into the bedroom and look out the window. Maybe we'll see something."

Madison followed Dino into the bedroom. She ran to the window and pulled up the blinds to complete darkness. After sliding open the window, Dino used his flashlight to look around. The first thing Madison noticed, the streets were filled with water. She slid another window open hearing water hitting the front of her house. Dino's flashlight acted as a spotlight. Stunned, she watched cars float down the street. People screaming with the sound of police sirens echoed in the far distance. Peering straight down, it looked as if their house sat in the center of a lake.

"When I said no distractions, I didn't mean to this extent."

"Oh Dino," she cried. "What are we going to do?"

"I wish I knew. This wasn't something in the game plan for today."

She reached her hand out. "Give me the flashlight. I want to check the stairs again."

"You're not going alone."

Madison held on tightly to Dino's hand. Taking a deep breath together, they slowly made their way down the hallway. Dino kept the light of the flashlight pointing straight. She suspected he was just as scared as her. Slowly he lowered the light. They both gasped at the same time. The water had risen up to the top step.

"Get back into the bedroom. Gather all your candles and matches. We need to make sure we have enough of light to get us through the night," Dino ordered.

"I can't do this."

"You will have to. We have to be alert. I don't know what is going on outside, but from the sound of the fire engines and police sirens, I don't think it's good. Now go."

Madison ran down the hall, back into their bedroom. She opened her drawers and took out the candles in the back of her drawers. Each drawer had four candles, one in each corner. Since she loved the aroma of vanilla, she had placed them throughout her drawers.

In her makeup vanity drawer, she took out an old cosmetic case and placed all the candles in the bag along with matches. In her nightstand she had a smaller flashlight, which she took out and turned on. Reaching for the landline, she then placed the receiver against her ear to hear no dial tone, only silence. She kept turning the phone off and on, getting the same results. Next, she grabbed her cell phone and let out a scream when no bars showed on the screen.

Dino returned to the room, his boxer shorts wet, sticking to his body. "This is serious, baby."

"What happened to you? Why are you all wet? What did you see?" she rambled.

"Oh baby, we are so screwed right now."

"How? Why?"

"Our downstairs is gone, flooded out, under water. I tried to go down the stairs, but I only could get down three steps. If I went down any farther, I would have had to start swimming."

"Oh God," she repeated over and over again. "We have no phone service at all. The landlines are out. So are the cell phones."

"Really?"

"I can't get in touch with Shari. I hate that I can't talk to her or hear her say everything is going to be okay. Are we, are my friends going to be okay?" Madison looked into Dino's eyes. "Please tell me everything is going to be okay. Please."

"I will protect you. I won't let anything at all happen to you. I can't promise you your friends will be okay."

Madison started breathing hard. This had turned into a nightmare. Their perfect afternoon had turned into a disastrous night. She turned to face Dino whose expression was blank. No doubt he shared the same fears as her, but didn't want to show it.

"What are we going to do?"

"I think we are going to have to go upstairs to the attic."

"The attic. Why?"

"Because the water is on this floor." Dino stood within inches of her. "Madison, I'm scared. For once in my life, I don't know what to do."

"We can't panic. But what is going to happen if the water goes up to the attic?"

"You know the prayer you are always saying every night for me?"

"Yes, the prayer to Saint Anthony."

"Start saying it for us."

"Why do you say that?"

"Because we are going to need it."

* * * *

Shari put Thomas to sleep. Quietly, she tiptoed out of the room and went to slip into her black negligee before walking into the living room. Tommy squatted in front of the fireplace, adding extra wood.

As the wind howled, the branches from the hundred year old oak tree in her backyard hit against the back of the house, directly over her octagon prayer room. Hopefully, the noise wouldn't wake Thomas because she had some plans for his daddy. The fire crackled as Tommy used a poker to push the wood around, chasing away the bad vibes from the storm.

"I can feel you staring at my ass," Tommy said without turning around.

"How'd you know?" Shari asked walking toward him.

Tommy stood, turning to face her. He grinned. "You smell luscious. Now you look...well..." He pointed to his erection.

"Hmm. Tell me more. I've wanted you from the moment I saw you on the ladder covering the windows. Your muscles were bulging out of your T-shirt."

"You sure know how to seduce me." Tommy walked over to her and ran his fingers down her arms. "How about I get a blanket, two bottles of beer along with the small tray of cheese and crackers you made earlier?"

"Sounds perfect."

Tommy kissed her before disappearing down the hall to their bedroom. Shari pushed the cocktail table back making enough room for Tommy to place the blanket.

"You need any help?" Shari asked walking toward the kitchen.

"No. I have everything under control. You do everything for me, so tonight it's my turn to return the favor."

"I'm not going to give you an argument."

Tommy returned with the blanket. "If you don't mind putting the blanket down, I'll go get our goodies."

Shari grinned. There wasn't going to be any drinking or eating, not just yet. She wanted to spend this quiet time with Tommy just in case Thomas woke up. Once she straightened the blanket out, she sat down in the center facing the fireplace.

"I'll be right with you," Tommy called into the living room.

Before she could answer, her doorbell rang. Who the hell would be here? *Screw it. I'm just going to ignore it. I'm not going to let anyone ruin my night with Tommy.* These nights are few and far in between. The last time they made love, Thomas came knocking on their bedroom door crying. So tonight, they'd make love first, then eat.

Whoever stood outside her door continued to ring the doorbell. This time she heard someone screaming for help. Strange. The voice sounded vaguely familiar.

"Baby, who's at the door?" Tommy asked from the doorway.

Shari stood. "I don't know. I'll go see." She took Tommy's sweat shirt off the couch, put it on and zipped it up. "I'm coming," she yelled as she walked down the stairs.

As she got closer to the door, she could still hear someone yelling for help from outside. She opened the door to Heather, who stood drenched from head to toe.

"Oh my God. What the hell happened to you?"

"Oh, Aunt Shari. It's a disaster. You wouldn't believe what's going on."

"Let's go upstairs to get you out of these wet clothes." Shari shut and locked the door behind them. "Why didn't you call me? I would've come to get you."

"There is no phone service. All the lines are down."

"Are you kidding me?" Shari asked following Heather.

"The hurricane. It knocked everything down. There's no lights, no landlines, no cell phones."

"What are you talking about?" Shari asked when they reached the top of the stairs.

"Jesus," Tommy said. "What happened to you?" He grabbed the blanket off the floor and wrapped it around Heather.

"The hurricane. One minute I was watching television, the next, water started gushing into my house." Heather looked around. "You have lights?"

"Yes. That's why I don't understand what you are talking about. Let me get dressed and get you dry clothes. Do you want to take a bath, shower?"

"No, Aunt Shari. I'm scared. The streets are filled with water. I'm lucky I got here. I had to walk through some of the streets with water up to my waist."

"Madison?" Shari reached for her landline. Nothing. Hands shaking, she lifted her handbag and emptied the contents out on the table.

Grabbing her cell phone, she tapped in Madison's number. "I'm sorry. All circuits are busy. Please try your call later."

"Oh dear God." She tapped in Madison's number again, getting the same message. "Where is the water in the streets, Heather?"

"All the streets by the shoreline are flooded out. The ocean's waves are breaking on the other side of the boulevard. The water is going straight up to Hylan Boulevard. I'm so scared."

"I'm going to get dressed. I have to go find Madison, Cassie and Sophia. Do you have a clue as to where they are?" Shari asked.

"No. I was about to ask you the same question."

Shari twirled her fingers through her hair. How could this happen? How could she not know where her friends were, especially Madison, her best friend. She had to find her.

Rushing off into the bedroom, she got out of her negligee and put on a pair of jeans and T-shirt. Opening another drawer, she took out a navy blue velvet sweat suit along with a white tank top and white sweat socks and underwear.

"Here you go." She handed Heather the clothes and started running down the stairs.

"Babe, where are you going? You can't go out there," Tommy called after her.

"Watch me."

Shari reached the bottom of the stairs. When she opened the door, the wind slapped her in the face, causing her to fall backward. She sat on the floor with her back leaning against the stairs. *Damn, what the hell just happened?* She tried to get up, and couldn't move her left leg.

"Tommy, I need help," she screamed. "I can't get up."

Shari leaned her head back watching Tommy come down the stairs toward her, with Heather following behind.

"Are you okay, Aunt Shari?"

"No. I can't move my leg," she cried. "The pain is unbearable."

Tommy turned to Heather. "Go upstairs, start making icepacks with the kitchen towels."

Shari heard Heather's footsteps rushing up the stairs. Before she could say a word, Tommy leaned down, scooped her into his arms, carried her up the stairs and into their bedroom. Heather appeared with two big ice packs wrapped in kitchen towels.

"I want you to stay here with Shari, make sure she doesn't move." Tommy reached for the remote control and turned the television on. "Thank God we have electricity so we can find out what's going on…"

All three of them stood in silence, with their eyes glued to the television. They were in the middle of a hurricane with eighty mile an hour winds and thirty-foot waves. From what Shari could comprehend, the whole city was the center of one of the biggest hurricanes that had taken place in over a hundred years. The more they watched, the more Shari knew the hurricane had been coming up in the cards for the past two weeks. The one thing she didn't expect was a total disaster, affecting millions of people.

"I'm going out to see what's going on." Tommy's left eye twitched, indicating his fear too.

"I don't want you to leave. I need you here with me. I am in so much pain. I think I broke my leg."

"I'm going to see if the streets are clear so I can get you to the hospital."

"You can't," Heather said. "They evacuated the hospital earlier today."

"I had no idea," Shari said. "I've been putting all my focus on Fay and Heather's shop since the fire. Honestly, I haven't listened to the news at all."

Shari tried to move her leg. "Damn," she shrilled. "The pain is horrendous."

"Stay with her," Tommy said to Heather. "Thomas should be down for the night. We don't need him to wake up to add to everything."

"Please be careful, Tommy."

Tommy leaned over, kissing her forehead. "I'll be back in a bit."

* * * *

The young girl sitting next to Fay nudged her. Fay opened her eyes. "We're home already? That was fast."

"No. The pilot made an emergency landing in London. While you were sleeping they made an announcement that all flights in and out of the east coast have been cancelled due to a hurricane."

"Are you kidding me? I have to get home. My vintage clothing shop was destroyed in a fire. I also have to make sure my daughter is okay and fill out paperwork."

"Doesn't look like you're going anywhere." The young girl stood. "We have to get off the plane. Do you want to get a martini in the bar?"

"Yes. But first I have to call, make sure my daughter is okay."

"I'm Lorraine."

"Nice to meet you. I'm Fay."

Fay followed Lorraine off the plane. Thank God she didn't deactivate her international phone card. She tapped Heather's cell phone number into her phone. "Sorry, all circuits are busy. Try again later," the recording said. She tried calling her house. The phone was busy. Strange. Especially since she had call waiting. After numerous attempts, she called Madison, then Shari and got the same results.

"What's wrong?" Lorraine asked.

Fay explained to her the results of her phone calls. "Something is wrong."

Lorraine pointed to the bar. "They have a television in there with the news on. Maybe we can find something out."

Fay slid onto the bar stool closest to the television.

"What can I get you?" the young bartender asked in a heavy British accent.

"Do you know what's going on?" she asked pointing to the television.

"Hurricane has hit the east coast. New York is getting blasted. There are already five fatalities on Staten Island. The ocean is slamming the coastline."

"I have to get home. I can't sit here not being able to contact my daughter or my friends."

Fay fled from the bar and ran across the airport to the departure board. Maybe she could get another flight into New York. However, the word cancelled in uppercase red letters read next to every fight leaving London to New York and New Jersey.

Dear God. How the hell am I going to get home to Heather?

Chapter Six

Cassie took a bite of her sandwich. "I've got to hand it to you, Antonio. This is the best grilled chicken, broccoli rabe and fresh mozzarella sandwich I've ever eaten. Where did you get it from?"

"There's a small mom and pop luncheonette behind the precinct. That's another reason why it took me so long. Everything they cook is to order. It's the best-kept secret. I got all the guys ordering from them."

"I think I'll be spending more time eating dinner with you. I bet they make their own mozzarella too." Cassie slid a piece of cheese out of her sandwich and fed it to Antonio.

"Delicious. But," he held up half his hero sandwich, "I'll take my chicken cutlet parmigiana any time over broccoli rabe. How can you eat that shit? It's so bitter."

"It's an acquired taste. I never liked it as a kid."

Cassie took a sip of her diet soda. "I love doing things like this."

"Wouldn't you rather be sitting in a restaurant with a glass of wine?"

"I want to be anywhere that includes you."

"That's what I like to hear," Antonio said with a mouthful. He finished chewing before reaching his hand out.

Cassie put her sandwich down before grabbing his hand. Taking his lead, Cassie stood, walked to Antonio's side of the desk and plopped on his lap. "That's how I truly feel. I'm sorry it took me so long to put my heart out to you."

"I understand."

"I can't thank you enough for your patience. I wasn't sure if I was ready to get into another relationship with anyone." Cassie stood.

"What made you change your mind?" Antonio took the last bite of his sandwich before cleaning up the mess except for the half of hero sandwich Cassie had left along with some French fries.

"I saw something different in you. Not the side your ex-wife marred you with when she had me serve you with that order of protection."

"I didn't deserve what she did to me."

"I know you didn't. What I see is a man who pays child support and goes the extra yard to make sure his kids are totally taken care of."

"That means a lot to me." Antonio took Cassie's hands in his. "I found my true love when I met you."

Cassie blinked her eyes, putting her head down.

"Look at you." He touched her face. "You're blushing."

"No one has ever said those words to me." Cassie looked up, catching his gaze. "I feel the same way."

"I'd like to get out of here. Take you home. Talk about moving our relationship a step further. Is this something you'd be interested in doing?"

Cassie parted her lips into a smile. "Yes. Of course you already met my family."

Antonio chuckled. "Next time my kids come over, we'll talk about the trip to Florida. I'll tell them you'll be coming along."

"I'd love that. I think I'm ready to become a part of your life."

Antonio gathered her in his arms, kissing the top of Cassie's head. "Things always have a way of working out." He stepped back, looked at his watch. "Geez, it's after eight. I wonder where O'Sullivan is. Let me call the desk. He loves strolling in and flirting with Weitz at the front desk. And believe me, she encourages it."

"I'm sure she does."

Antonio lifted the receiver. Immediately, he placed it back down in the cradle and repeated the process. "That's strange. No dial tone."

"Try your cell phone. Maybe all the wind knocked the phone lines down." Cassie pointed toward the window. "The phone lines are above ground. Look at the wires swaying back and forth."

Flipping open his phone, he punched the numbers in. He closed it, shaking his head side to side. "That's strange. Circuits are busy. I'm going to walk down the hall to see what's going on. I'll also grab us some coffee." He pointed to the windowsill. "I have some cookies and red velvet cupcakes in the box."

"Yummy. Red velvet, my favorite." She lifted the box up. "I'll set up our mini dessert buffet while you're gone."

"Perfect."

Cassie pulled at the thin red and white string on the box. Just as she started to slide the string off, Antonio yelled, "Holy shit."

Twirling around, she stared at Antonio. "What's wrong?"

"Look." He pointed to the floor. "I'm standing in a puddle of water. Where the hell did that come from?"

"I have no idea."

Antonio went over to the window facing the squad room and pulled up the blind. "Cassie, come here. You're not going to believe this."

Cassie walked through the water seeping in under the door. "Damn, this is disgusting. You don't think the toilet down the hall overflowed, do you?"

"Look at this. Unless the whole sewer system backed up, I doubt the toilet overflowed."

"Don't be ridiculous—" Cassie's mouth dropped open. "The water is gushing down the hall like a river." She pushed her hair behind her ears to stop the loose strands from falling in her eyes. "Antonio, where is the water coming from?"

"I don't know. I'll walk down the hall to see."

"No, you can't do that. If you open the door more water is going to come rushing into the room," she said, her words blending together.

"Baby, I have to see what's going on, if anyone needs my help."

"I don't—"

As Antonio opened the door, the water came gushing in. Quickly, the room filled with two feet of water.

"Oh my God. The room is filling up." Cassie stuck her head out the door. The water continued to flow down the hall with articles of office supplies floating on the top.

"Go back in the office. I'll be right back."

"Please don't leave me," Cassie cried.

"Hello. Is anyone there?" Antonio yelled from the door.

"Yes. But we are stuck inside. The water is so high. We are standing on our desks here. Stay put," she heard someone yell from down the hall. "Are you guys okay?"

"As okay as we can be."

Antonio walked back into the room and forced the door closed, sighing in relief. "This isn't good. We have to find a way out of here."

Cassie walked to the window. Attached to the sash hung a big silver padlock. The one Shari had mentioned months ago. By chance, she pulled on the lock, hoping it would pop open, but to no avail.

Turning around to face Antonio, she asked, "Do you have the key?"

"What key?"

"The key to the padlock, Antonio."

"How the hell do I know where it is?"

"Don't you remember the day Shari stopped by? You said you knew where the key was. Well where the hell is it?"

"I don't know," he screamed, his face turning crimson.

Cassie froze in place. The look on Antonio's face said it all. He had become pissed at her insistence.

Her eyes remained on him as they stared at each other in silence. If she would have been able to walk out of the office, she would have been gone, out of his life. His tone scared her. This situation scared the hell out of her. She expected him to offer his comfort and support. Yelling left her insides cold. His tone reminded her of her ex-husband of many years ago. She dropped her gaze from his and climbed up on the windowsill. One way or another she was going to get out of there.

"What the hell are you doing?"

"Trying to figure out how we are going to get the hell out of here. If the water keeps rising, we will drown in a matter of an hour or two."

Antonio walked to the window, reaching his hand out to her. "Get down from there. The key has to be in my drawer. Between the two of us we can find it."

Cassie took his hand, allowing him to help her down. "Are you sure it's in the drawer?" she asked searching his expression for a positive response.

"Absolutely not. The padlocks were put on the windows years ago when a prisoner escaped. It never crossed my mind I would ever need to remove them."

"That's great. Don't you guys have a contingency plan in the event of a fire, a shootout or a hostage situation?"

"Baby, this isn't television. Sure something like that could possibly happen, but the chances are close to nil. Right now we have to figure out where I put the key. Let's go through the desk." He pulled open the top drawer and put it on top of the desk.

Cassie took things out one at a time, making certain she went through every piece of paper and notebook, coming up empty.

"Nothing in this drawer except notebooks, pens and stationery supplies."

Antonio used his hand to slide the contents of the drawer into the water, which had raised another half a foot. He placed another drawer filled with files in front of her.

"Two drawers down."

They continued to go through the second set of drawers, coming up empty again. Cassie looked down. She had felt the water rising up her body, but just ignored it. The water had already reached her hips and they were no closer to finding the key than when they started out.

"Antonio, what the hell are we going to do," her voice shrieked.

"I don't know," he lashed out. "I can't remember where I put the damn key. I remember saying this is a good place to keep it. Now, I can't remember." He slammed the metal drawer down on his desk.

Cassie held her hand up. "Okay. We can't lose our cool. We have to stay calm."

"Calm? I need to find the key. If the water continues rising at this rate it will be up to the ceiling in a couple of hours. We will be dead."

Fear became evident in Antonio's voice. Cassie made her way back to the window and kneeled on the radiator. Reaching between the bars, she tried to open the window, but it was sealed shut. Outside, the water in the streets rushed past the precinct faster than earlier. Even if the window opened, there wasn't anywhere to go. The undertow of the water would carry them away, back into the harbor—then the Atlantic Ocean.

"Forget it, Antonio. We are so screwed," she murmured, turning around to face him.

"No we're not."

"Come look out the window."

"Dear God. I could swim faster to you than walk."

Cassie watched Antonio tread water with his arms as he struggled toward her. "Come up on the radiator. The water hasn't reached up here yet."

Antonio reached his leg up onto the radiator to stand next to Cassie. "Holy shit, look at the water rushing down the street. This is serious Cassie. What the hell are we going to do?"

"I don't know." She shook her head side to side. "We have to figure a way out of here."

"How? The hall is probably three feet already."

Cassie held the lock in her hand. "Can't you shoot this off?"

"I can, but where are we going to go. The water is rising outside the building too."

"What's above us?" She pointed to the ceiling.

"A few conference rooms, the captain's office."

Cassie looked around the room and stopped when she spotted a wrought iron square grate above his desk. This would be a long shot, Antonio would also think she was crazy, but this might be their only way out.

"We need to open the metal grate." She pointed. "It's our only way out."

"I don't know. I have no idea where it leads."

"I'd go with the floor above. It's worth a try," Cassie argued. "We have to do something or else we are both going to drown."

* * * *

Sophia held tightly onto the chandelier. Slowly, she opened her eyes and looked around. The room had turned into a lake. Table and chairs were on their sides, while place settings lay on the floor. The pink cloth napkins and the artificial flower centerpieces she had made floated around aimlessly.

Out of the corner of her eye, she saw the man, the one in the bright orange jacket who had warned her to go back into the building, floating head down in the water. A shiver raced through her. This had to be a dream she'd wake up from and find herself with her head down sleeping on her desk.

The sound of fire engines and police sirens were coming from the front of the building. She could hear someone talking on a megaphone. It was hard to make out the words because the voice was too far away. She wondered if she yelled help, if anyone would hear her. No one knew she had stayed at work except for Scott.

Turning around on the chandelier, she looked out toward the ocean. The windows were all blown out. Sophia squeezed her eyes closed and slowly opened them. This had to be a nightmare. The beach—the equivalent of two city blocks—had been replaced by water. And the boardwalk had at least six inches of water on its surface, meaning the basement/storage space for the catering hall had been flooded out.

"Help," she screamed, over and over again. Why she yelled, she didn't know because it would be impossible for anyone to hear her cries with the sound of ambulances now passing by in the distance.

Sophia took a deep breath. Think positive, her therapist had told her many years ago. The smell of the salt water calmed her, transporting her back in time. When she had graduated from grammar school her mom had taken her to Coney Island. It had been just the two of them to celebrate her graduating with a ninety-seven average. Those days seemed like only yesterday.

To think her own kid would have been close to twenty-eight years old. Why did she have an abortion all those years ago? Why didn't she just stand up to her parents and Cassie? That had always been her problem. She always looked for their approval. Since she'd been on her own, she had survived. And the day Scott walked into her life, a whole new world opened up for her. Things were finally starting to fall into place. After getting out of this mess, one of her main concerns would be going back to her house in Allentown, to finish destroying the letters she had started burning. No one could find or read them.

She had changed, become a totally different person. Thoughts of committing suicide would never take over her life again. Most people obsessed about their weight, Sophia obsessed about dying. But back then, she didn't have anything to live for. She was always the odd one in school, and in after school activities. The girl everyone made fun of. She proved everyone wrong when she started her own business, escaping from her parent's control and Cassie's opinions.

The last thing she wanted to do was drown. This situation did nothing for her fear of the ocean though. She just had to put this anxiety to rest so she could figure a way out of this disaster. Looking down again, she saw the stranger had floated across the room. Why couldn't he float out the broken windows? Glancing around again, she noticed the water had started to recede. If she jumped down, she would be able to land on a table no longer covered by water.

Ice ran through her veins. No one there to help her, daylight almost gone, she had to make a decision on the right way to get herself out of the chandelier in order to save herself. If she made a mistake, it would mean her life.

Sophia readjusted her full hundred and thirty-five pounds on the chandelier, surprised, it held her weight. Whoever hung it did some hell of a job supporting the fixture into a beam, probably a metal beam at that.

Dear God, why does the stranger have to keep floating underneath me. She took this as a good sign. This meant the water stopped gushing into the hall. Maybe this was the time to try to get out of there.

Her incentive in getting down would be to get back to her office so she could call Scott and warn him something bad had happened down at the beach. Even the wind seemed to have calmed down. She needed to pull herself together, not go back to her old ways. Keeping her cool would be of extreme importance.

Oh God, the girls. She wondered if they were okay. Another incentive for her to get the hell out of here. Since they all lived within a mile of each other, she would drive by each of their houses to check on them.

Okay Sophia, enough thinking. Time to make a move and stop procrastinating. I know I can do this. I have to.

She sat on the thick glass chandelier, which was the shape of a half moon. Slowly, she dropped her hold. Closing her eyes, she started counting. "One, two, two and a half...go." The cold metal of the chandelier bit into her hand again as she grabbed onto her lifeline.

I have to take a deep breath and let go. I am so scared of the water, but it's my only escape. Let's do this one more time. "One, two..." This time Sophia let go. The three feet of water caught her fall. Quickly, she scrambled to her feet, the water covering her thighs. The tops of all the tables were now visible, which she hoped meant the water had started receding.

Sand and debris covered the charcoal gray and burgundy rug. Floating on top of the water were syringes, plastic bottles, paper along with other unidentifiable objects. The stench left her feeling nauseous. She had two alternatives to play with. One would be she walked out onto the boardwalk, or the other she got herself to the front of the building. Looking out at the boardwalk all she saw was sand, water and wood floating. Taking this into consideration her best bet would be to escape to the front of the building, where she could get into her car and get the hell out of there.

Pushing open the doors to the hallway turned into a huge challenge. The water on the other side held them tightly closed. Walking along the back of the hall, she made her way to the French doors on the opposite side, which led into the cocktail hour room. That might be her only way out. When she reached the doors, she knew exactly what she needed to do.

Reaching down, she lifted the metal water pitcher off the floor. Sophia's adrenaline went into overdrive when she spun around and threw it. With her back to the doors, she heard the glass shatter, then felt a sharp pain in her upper right arm. Looking down, she saw a piece of glass wedged into her triceps. *Blood. Oh my God, blood. I'm going to pass out.* She took a deep breath. *No. I have to keep in control if I want to get out of this place in one piece.*

Sophia lifted a pink cloth napkin off the floor and wrung it out. She pulled the piece of glass from her skin before wrapping the napkin around her wound. Time was of the essence to get out of here so she could drive herself directly to the hospital. But first she had to get out of there.

Using the metal pitcher, she broke the wood that had held the glass panes in place. She knew this wasn't going to be an easy feat. The hallway was filled with debris and food floating in the water. *I need to concentrate, not look down. Between seeing the food, along with the stench, I want to throw up. I have to keep myself together.*

Sirens went off in the distance. She couldn't understand why she didn't hear people or cars. She had a feeling something wasn't right. What was she going to find when she got out to the street side of the building? And would she ever get to the other side of the building with all this water and closed doors?

When she hit the main hallway, she felt water dripping down on her. She looked up. The skylight ceiling was totally gone, wiped out. All the furniture in the lobby was gone along with the marble table, which usually held the place cards. The front doors were blown out along with the glass windows.

This couldn't be happening. This was something you saw on the news or in a television movie. Could it be the meteorologist on the morning news wasn't joking about this storm? She should have listened instead of blowing the warnings off. But then again, she would have done the same exact thing. She still would have stayed at work while she waited for Scott to return from Allentown.

Scott. She had to get home to him. Looking down, she had to be very careful where she stepped. There was glass all over the place. The last thing she needed was to get a piece of glass stuck in her foot. Slowly she walked toward the open entrance.

She gasped. "Oh my God."

Her eyes bulged open. The streets were totally wiped out. Father Capodanno was flooded out with sand lining the streets. Two of the houses across the street from the catering hall were gone, while another one had moved completely off its concrete foundation and sat in the middle of the street.

Sophia walked onto the deck. The only thing she saw were bright lights coming from down the road. The street lights were out, the houses up the block completely dark, meaning there was a blackout. She needed to get the flashlight in her office. Good thing her office was in the front of the building. Just the thought of going back into that water filled mess frightened her, but she had no other choice. In less than a half-hour the sun would set leaving complete darkness except for the full moon, which would be hidden behind the clouds.

"I can do this." She kept repeating those words as she walked through the water down the hall to her office. The door had been ripped off the hinges, her desk lay on its side. Treading through the water, pains shot through her feet and up her body. She wanted to stop, take a break, but knew time wasn't on her side.

Darkness filled the room as she got to her credenza. Something hit her leg and she let out a scream. *I need to focus. I know the flashlight is on the top shelf. I'll just have to be careful looking around until I find it.*

She held onto the door with one hand while feeling her way around with the other, coming up empty. *I got to take my time. I'm rushing, causing me to miss it.*

Sophia took a deep breath and started from the right, working her way to the left. Just when she thought she was screwed, her hand landed on a thick string. That's when she remembered the day she had tied the red and black rope onto the small round hook so in an emergency she could wear the flashlight around her neck. Her colleagues all laughed at her. Boy was she happy she brushed them off.

Placing the rope around her neck, she slid the switch up. "Yes." She clinched her fist in triumph. Many years ago, she had remembered her photography teacher telling her to always change the small disk battery in her camera the beginning of every season. That always remained in her mind. So every season, she changed the batteries in her flashlights, smoke and carbon monoxide detectors and kitchen clock. The camera battery was obsolete, but the words of wisdom always remained in her head. She had yet to forget a season.

Sophia held the flashlight straight, lighting the path in front of her. Her clothes were wet, her shoes and socks saturated. The path back to the deck had become blocked with a round table that had apparently floated into the hall. Now she had to figure out a way around the table. Taking a deep breath, she looked at her two options. She either swam under the table or climbed over it. The thought of holding her breath and swimming in the dirty, debris-filled water made her decision easier. She'd take her chances climbing over the table.

Chapter Seven

Madison sat cross-legged on a quilt in the center of the crawl space in the attic with Dino by her side. The past half-hour they heard water swishing outside and inside the house. A few minutes earlier the wind stopped howling, leaving the sound of the water not as pronounced. She squeezed Dino's hand.

"Are you okay?" she asked, leaning over kissing his cheek.

"Yes. I must admit I feel better since the wind died down. I can totally go for a beer."

"I'm sure you can." Madison grinned. "But that isn't going to happen anytime soon. I think we should be content in having bottled water."

"And where are you getting water from?"

"I have a case of water in the closet along with some munchies."

"Munchies? Tell me where. I'll go down to get them."

"No. I want you to stay up here."

"No way. I'm supposed to be taking care of you, not the opposite way around."

Madison lifted her hand up. "I almost lost you. That's a feeling I don't ever want to feel again. The doctor says you are to be in a stress free environment. I don't think you walking down those rickety wooden steps is going to make your mini journey stress free. Please let me go do this."

"I don't feel right letting you do this. You must promise me you won't do anything that will put your life in jeopardy."

"It's a promise. Maybe our cell phones will be up and running, so I can make sure everyone is okay."

"Just be careful. If things look dangerous, you are to come right back up here."

"Promise."

Before she stood, Madison kissed Dino. She let him hold onto her hand until she had to push the stairs down. Her flashlight pointing out the way, she slowly walked down the creaky stairs. The silence in the house was deafening. Her house always had music playing, candles lit and smelled of a pot of freshly brewed coffee. What she wouldn't give to pinch herself to wake up from this disastrous dream. That's what it had to be. No way would something like this really happen in Staten Island. She wanted everything to go away, back to the way things were.

Water lapped at her toes, causing a chill to run through her body. The icy depths had risen a quarter of the way up the stairs. Shining the flashlight down, she saw dark muddy ripples where her hardwood floors used to be. A few feet in front of her, papers floated among other odds and ends. The light exposed pages of the press releases she had written the night before.

Her thoughts immediately raced to Dino's music room. If all her papers floated up here, then that meant his music room had been destroyed also. Madison took a deep breath. She had to be strong, not let Dino know how bad things really were.

"Baby is everything all right down there?"

"Yes Dino, just a lot of water," she answered, walking to the bottom of the attic steps.

Dino's concerned face stared back at her when she looked up. How could she tell him if the water didn't stop rising, they would both be dead? There was nowhere else to go. Why didn't she take the warning seriously. All morning long there were special reports telling people who lived in flood zone A to evacuate. But Dino wanting to make love to her for the first time in months took priority. She put all thoughts of the hurricane out of her mind.

"Are you okay, sweetheart? You seem to have zoned out."

"I'm fine." Madison managed a quick grin. "Let me go get a couple of things. I'll be right back."

"Before you come up, can you grab my medicine off the nightstand?"

"Yes. Your medicine is very important. I hope you have enough in the bottles to last a couple of days."

"Couple of days? What are you talking about?"

"Dino, downstairs is all flooded. We can't get out our front door."

"I'm coming down."

"No." She held up her hand. "Stay put. I'll be right there."

Madison made her way into their bedroom. She tried the house phone, and then the cell phone. There was still no service on either. Water was about an inch below the top of the mattress. Reaching down, she discovered it was completely saturated. She jumped back when something cold hit her leg. Unfortunately, her feet slipped out from under her, and down she went into the cold water, letting out a scream.

"What happened?" Dino's voice carried down the stairs.

"I lost my footing and got soaked," Madison said, using the bed to stand up.

"I'm coming down there."

"No you're not," she yelled. "I'm grabbing your medicine and getting dry clothes from the closet. I'll be up there in a few minutes."

"Hurry up. I'm freezing up here. I need your body heat."

Madison giggled nervously. Shining the flashlight around the room, she spotted a few candles literally floating on top of the water along with the papers that had drifted up from Dino's studio. Dino couldn't come down here. If he knew all the stuff from his studio was coasting through the hallway, into their bedroom, that would be all the stress needed to cause him to get chest pains.

At the closet, she pulled out the metal stepstool. After opening it up, she carefully climbed up to the top step and took down the waterproof beach bag that still sat on the shelf. Thank God, she didn't put away any of the summer gear. From one of the decorative boxes on the shelf, she took out a sweat shirt for herself and one for Dino. Quickly, she grabbed a pair of velvet sweat pants for herself. Since the nightstand was submerged in water, she wasn't going to be able to retrieve another pair of underwear. She grabbed a new package of briefs from the shelf and threw them in the bag, along with their sneakers.

She lifted the cover from another box, and put a bag of pretzels, along with some cheese doodle packets plus two cookies and cream candy bars in her beach bag. The last thing she added were four bottles of water off the shelf.

Carefully, she stepped off the stool holding the beach bag high, making certain not to let it touch the water. Dino's medicine wasn't on the nightstand. *Damn it. I am not going upstairs without his pills.*

Madison struggled through the water, with the beach bag wrapped around her neck. The flashlight lit the water. She found one of the medicine bottles on the opposite side of the room. After carefully skimming the water again, she found another one near their hot tub with the third bottle by the top of the stairs. Reaching out, she held onto the railing while using her foot to kick the bottle toward her. She had to get that bottle. Dino's life depended on him taking all his medication.

"Madison, what the hell are you doing?"

Madison turned around, bottle in hand. Dino stood halfway down the stairs shining the flashlight at her.

"I'm coming now. I just had to get your medicine bottles."

"By the top of the stairs?"

"Yes," she answered.

At the bottom of the stairs, she pulled the bag off and handed it to Dino. She sighed in relief. It had felt like a twenty pound weight around her neck. Distracted with rubbing her neck, Madison missed the top step and slipped. Grabbing onto the steps, she stopped herself from tumbling back down, the last thing she needed. Dino needed her. She had to take care of him. Whatever was going on outside, she wouldn't know until the morning when daylight would give them the light they needed to see. But for tonight, they would have to get through this together.

A cluster of helicopters flew overhead while the sirens of emergency vehicles echoed in the distance. Daylight would hold the key to exactly what was going on. Madison shivered as cold air settled into her bones. The first thing she needed to do was get out of her wet clothes.

"Here, let me help you." Dino slid her sneakers off. "Did you get a dry pair of socks?"

"No. The nightstand is totally submerged in water."

As Dino looked up at her, her frayed nerves finally got the best of her. She teared up, not knowing what lay ahead for them. Every one of her possessions was ruined. All they had left were memories. She felt bad for Dino. All his equipment had been destroyed. No way anything downstairs would have survived the water.

"Come on, baby, you need to stay warm." Dino kissed her cheek, holding dry clothes ready for her to slip into. Here she thought Dino needed her, when in reality she needed him.

"No thong?" he asked looking in the bag.

"No. Hope you don't mind, I took a package of your briefs for both of us to use."

"Not in the least."

Once Madison was fully dressed, she pointed to the blanket and two quilts Dino had set up. "Where did you find these?"

"In the box labeled to be donated."

"You never took them?" Madison asked lying down on the makeshift bed.

"Thank God I didn't, otherwise we would be sleeping on the plywood floor."

Madison held her hand out to Dino who sat with his legs spread in front of him. "I'm scared, Dino. What if we can't get out of here?"

"We will. But you have to keep a positive attitude."

"I'm trying to."

"Hey." Dino gathered her into his arms, holding her tightly. "I know we are in big trouble. I saw the water. I know my studio is destroyed. But all my records are saved in cyber space. Everything you worked on last night is saved. When we get out of here, we'll get another computer."

"But we lost everything."

Dino covered her lips with his index finger. "No we didn't lose everything."

"But you didn't see what I saw from the top of the steps."

"No, I didn't." Dino kissed the top of her head. "While you were downstairs, I had tears in my eyes too. I knew the reason why you didn't want me to come down with you is because you wanted to protect me from seeing everything destroyed. But I'm not a fool. The last thing I did before I called down to you was thank God the most important person in my life wasn't taken from me. I don't think I could ever survive if you weren't a part of my life."

"Oh Dino, I feel the same. I love you so much. You are right. I didn't lose everything. I still have the one thing money can't buy. Your love."

* * * *

Shari opened her eyes. This is what she had been doing since the pain had become unbearable. The best thing to do was for her to sleep through it. Tommy had given her three aspirins to take, but she really needed a heavy-duty painkiller. The ones the doctors warn you that you could become addicted too. No herbal vitamin or yellow candle could take away this pain.

Again, Shari tried again to get off her bed, but the pain shook her whole body. You didn't have to be a doctor to know her leg was either broken or fractured. She knew as soon as she fell, the pain was immediate. Now she was immobile. No way would she be able to make it up the stairs to her altar. She needed to light her candles and read her tarot cards.

Shari picked the remote control off the bed and turned the television on. Each channel had coverage of the hurricane. Patiently, she waited to see the segment on Staten Island. Reporter Holly Logan came on dressed totally out of character. The blonde hair, well-dressed reporter stood in a yellow raincoat that reminded her of the one her mother had dressed her in when she had been a kid, accompanied by a baseball cap.

"I'm here in Staten Island on Hylan Boulevard." The camera panned down to her feet, showing her in yellow rubber boots up to her knees, with the water barely a half an inch from the top, before returning to a full body shot. "This is as close to the beach as we could get. The streets below the boulevard are flooded with water levels as high as six feet." Holly pointed over her shoulder with the camera following her finger. "Hylan Boulevard toward the Verrazano Bridge is a lake. Most of the coastal line is under water…" The reporter hesitated for a few moments. "We have been advised to leave the area. Go to higher ground. We'll get back to you when we get settled. I'm Holly Logan reporting from Hylan Boulevard in Staten Island. Back to you, Scott and Brook."

Shari covered her mouth with her hands. *Dear God.* Tommy went out to see if Madison was okay. Now she had to worry about both of them. "Heather," she called out, not wanting to yell and wake up Thomas. She waited a few minutes before calling out to her again. This time Heather appeared in the doorway.

"Do you need something, Aunt Shari? I just put up a pot of coffee."

"Yes. I need for you to do me a huge favor since I can't get up."

"Sure. I'll bring you your cup of coffee."

"Before you do that, I need for you to go up in the attic to get me a couple of things."

"Your tarot cards?"

"Yes to start. I also need a clear altar dish, four white candles, my purple scarf and the long white wooden matches."

"Okay. I'll be right back."

The scent of the coffee filled the room. Shari tried to move her leg, but as soon as she did pain shot all the way up her hip. With no cell phone, she had no way of contacting Tommy or Madison to make sure they were all right. Never in her whole life did she ever feel so out of sorts.

Heather's footsteps were directly over her head, as the floor creaked every time she moved. She knew exactly what Heather was doing just by the sound above. Within a few minutes, she handed Shari the tarot cards and placed the rest of the supplies on the bed in arms reach.

"I'll go get your coffee. Do you want something to eat?"

"Nah, I'm okay. I'm in no mood for anything. I know everyone is going to be okay. I just need to hear from them."

Tears rolled down Heather's cheeks. "I'm so scared, Aunt Shari. My mom is on her way home. I don't know where she is. Her flight had left according to schedule, but now there is no information on where the flight landed or if the plane is still in the air."

Shari held her hand out to Heather. "Come sit here."

Heather sat, resting her head on Shari's shoulder, still crying.

Shari put her arms around her and cradled her. "I'm just as afraid as you are," Shari admitted. "From what I'm seeing on television, everything is flooded out by Aunt Madison. I doubt she evacuated."

"Maybe she did."

"If she did, she would be right here with us. I feel that Madison and Dino are okay, but they are in some sort of trouble. I can't put my finger on it."

"You don't think her house was hit, do you?" Heather asked, sitting up.

"They live a half a mile away from the water. I doubt the flood levels made it up to them."

"Me and my mom lost everything. First our store, now our house."

As Heather stared at her, she reached out, touched her head and closed her eyes.

I can't believe this is happening. I lost everything. There is nothing left at all of my childhood. The store, which was the core of our family for so many generations, is burned down, leaving us with no business.

I left my house because the water started coming in. I bet by now the water has destroyed the first floor. My house is only four blocks from the ocean. From what I saw on the news, it looks like the whole beach community has been washed out.

Oh God. If anything happens to my mother, I could never live with myself. I need her. I love her. I can't lose her.

Shari opened her eyes. Tears trickled down her cheeks. This time they weren't tears of pain, they were tears of worry. She wished she could channel into Fay, but she couldn't, she never could. Too much was going on in the universe for her to zero in on her friends. She needed to be there for Heather, assuring her everything would be okay.

"What's wrong, Aunt Shari?" she asked, handing her a tissue.

"I'm just worried, like you." She couldn't let Heather know she had read her mind. No sense in freaking her out.

"Let me get your coffee. I know you want to do your thing with the cards and candles." Heather half smiled.

Shari knew her nerves were getting the best of her.

"Maybe they will say something on TV about the flights. I'm sure wherever she is, she is safe."

"Thanks, Aunt Shari."

Heather returned within a few minutes with a cup of coffee along with two biscottis. Shari couldn't help but laugh. "Thanks, Heather."

"You're welcome. I'm going to sit in the living room. If you need me, just give me a holler."

The minute Heather left the room, Shari went to work. With her left hand, she slid over her nightstand to the side of the bed. She laid out the scarf, placed the clear dish in the center and put the candles in the small holders. After sliding open the top drawer, she took out a white pillar candle and set it in the middle of the dish. She was halfway there.

From the purple and gold drawstring bag, Shari took out a black, gray and white scarf. She laid the scarf on the bed and carefully unwrapped her deck of tarot cards. Closing her eyes, she held the cards close to her chest.

Water. I see water surrounding all my friends. I feel they are okay, but not safe. Why do I see them all trapped in a tight space? Fear is all around them, especially Sophia. She's in trouble with no one to help her.

Shari opened her eyes. This had to be a dream. How could she have fallen? Now she couldn't go out to help find her friends. She placed her tarot cards on the table and lifted her cell phone to try calling Madison again. The same recording played, saying all circuits were busy. "Damn it." She tossed her cell phone next to her. "This can't be happening."

Shari took a lighter from the nightstand drawer and turned off the television. Now the room was lit by candlelight. Lifting the cards, she started to shuffle them. Every time she stopped, she felt she had to keep on shuffling. The cards just didn't feel right in her hands. When a feeling of peace swept her body, she stopped. She placed the cards on the table, then cut them in three with her left hand before putting them back together.

The first card she turned over in the past position was *The Death* card. That card made sense in that position. In the past, each of her friends made major decisions regarding their relationships. Each of them resolved past relationships, moved on with another, resulting in happiness. So this was the appropriate card for the position.

Next, she would reveal the card in present position. Turning the card over, she uncovered *The Tower* card. Her mouth dropped open. This wasn't good. Disaster surrounded all of them. She felt their fear. There wasn't a single thing she could do to help them, trapped in bed, with Tommy somewhere out in the storm, with no line of communication at all.

Shari circled her fingers through her hair. This was becoming too hard to bear. In the distant, she heard the sound of fire engines and ambulances. The sirens' echoes sent chills through her.

Staring at the deck, she turned over *The Moon* card. Shari covered her face with her hands. This couldn't be happening. Whatever was going on outside, couldn't be something that affected them for the long haul. Or could it? God, how much trouble could a little wind and rain bring?

Shari lit the white candle in the middle. "I ask the universe to watch over my friends, keep them safe and bring us all back together. I hate being here unable to help my friends in need. Please watch over them, bring my husband safely back to me. So mote it be."

After rolling her neck side to side, Shari gathered her cards and wrapped them back in the scarf. Again, she tried to move her leg, but the pain surged throughout her body. No use in trying to move. When Tommy got home she would ask him to bring her to the hospital.

She heard the bells on the door downstairs ring. "Heather," she called out. "Who's at the door?"

Heather appeared in the doorway. Before she spoke Tommy called out, "It's me."

"Oh thank God. I was so worried about you. And my leg, I can't move. The pain is horrific. Heather, would you mind watching Thomas while I go to the hospital?"

"Slow down." Tommy appeared in the doorway, drenched from head to toe holding his work boots.

"What the hell happened to you? I thought it stopped raining."

"Oh baby, you can't imagine what is going on out there."

"Get out of those wet clothes. Talk to me."

"I'll go check on Thomas," Heather said, closing the door behind her.

Tommy pulled his shirt over his head. "Everything is flooded out there. The streets are a lake a half a mile from here. I just helped two other men rescue a woman from her house."

"What happened? Her house on fire?"

"No. The water gushed through her house, forcing her to climb out on the small wooden balcony on the side. It's a disaster area out there. I've never seen anything like I just saw in my whole entire life. Houses down by the beach have literally been washed away. People are stuck in their houses. The fire department is out there trying to rescue people by boat."

"By boat?" Shari asked, pulling her head back.

Tommy stepped out of his clothes and slid on a pair of dry sweat pants. "The streets are flooded out." He sat on the bed next to her. "Looks more like a battle zone out there."

"I feel so helpless."

"There's nothing you can do except to pray people get rescued. No one took this storm seriously. Now, all we can do is hope there are no casualties."

Tommy squeezed her hand. "How's the leg?"

"Bad. Very bad."

"I'll have Heather bring you in a couple of aspirins."

"Why not you? I thought you would sit with me for a while."

"I can't." Tommy shook his head. "I have to go back out to help."

Shari put her head down. "I understand."

"You are safe." He kissed her forehead. "There are families stuck in their houses, some with children. I'm going to go back out to help the firemen."

"I love you. Please be careful."

"I love you too."

* * * *

Fay kept her eyes glued to the television. The storm had hit the east coast hard, real hard. The British anchor announced all airports on the east coast were closed. Air traffic had come to a complete halt. Aerial pictures were being shown of the areas. When pictures of Staten Island were shown, Fay's mouth dropped open. The homes by the beach were completely submerged in water, with some torn off their foundations.

"Excuse me." Fay waved the bartender over. "Where can I find a computer?"

"There's a computer station down the hallway," he explained in a heavy English accent. "It's always crowded.

Today people can't live without having access to their computers."

"I can. But I need to get on to watch a local New York news channel to see exactly what's going on in Staten Island. My daughter and all my friends live there. All the phones are down. I can't talk to anyone to check in."

"Give me a minute," the tall slim bartender said. "I'll be right back."

Before Fay could reply, he walked into the back room. *Strange.* Just as Fay stood to walk down the hall, the bartender returned with his laptop.

"Here you go." He placed the laptop in front of her. "I'm Timothy." He extended his hand.

Fay shook his hand. "Fay."

"Nice to meet you. Please," he pointed to the laptop, "help yourself. I hope your family is safe."

"Thank you."

Fay turned the computer on and went directly to channel five. What she watched on the screen brought tears to her eyes. Home videos showed the devastation in various areas on the coast of New Jersey and New York. The anchor kept talking about zone A being evacuated.

After opening another tab, she put her street address in. Her house sat right in the middle of zone A. Tears rolled down her cheek. She had to know if her daughter was okay. But as she watched the news, it became clear the only way she would find out if Heather was safe would be to get on the next flight out. She needed to get back to the United States. Then she could continue her journey back home by car.

Fay closed the laptop. "Thank you," she said, handing it back to the bartender. "I'm going to see if I can get a flight back to the states."

"Flights are all cancelled."

"I will be on the next flight out of this airport. Trust me."

Chapter Eight

Cassie and Antonio stood on his desk staring up at the thick metal grating. Just by looking at the size of the hole, Cassie became extremely doubtful either one of them would be able to make it up and into it. From the look of things, there didn't seem to be anything solid to hold onto. The dark space reminded her of a laundry chute.

"Now what are we going to do?" Cassie cried, pointing to the rusted screws.

"I'm going to remove them. We'll take it from there."

"How are we going to make it up there?" she asked as dread filled her. "We're dead. I know it."

Antonio placed both his hands on her shoulders, shaking her. "You have to stay in control. I can't lose you now."

"Please, I'm so scared. I don't want to die. I want to see my friends, and make love to you. This can't be happening."

"Sh." He covered her lips with his finger. "I love you. I will get us out of here, I promise."

Cassie kept her eyes on Antonio as he used the pocketknife from his pocket to open the screws. After listening to him swear under his breath over a dozen times, one of the screws finally gave way. He pulled down the grating on one side before shining his flashlight up the opening.

"Hello. Anyone up there?" he yelled.

"Yes. O'Sullivan, Troy, Harris and Crystal."

"Palencia down here with my girlfriend, Cassie."

"What's it like down there?" a male voice echoed down.

"Water is brimming over my desk, with its level still rising. We need to get up the chute."

"What can we do to help?" the same man asked.

"Do you have rope up there?"

"Yes. A very thick twine. It's old, but I'm sure it will be able to hold up."

"Send it down. Make sure you tie your end tightly to something stationary. We can't afford to make any mistakes," Antonio explained.

"Give us a few minutes to get set up."

Antonio turned to Cassie. "I want you to know I'm just as scared. I'm not even sure I can fit in the chute."

"I'm not going without you."

"Baby, you are going first. My main concern is your safety. I know I can make it up the grating. I'll just take another dip into the water, lube myself up and I'll just slide right up there right after you."

"You are so optimistic."

"You have to be if you want to get out of here alive."

"Here you go." The rope dropped out of the hole. "Did you get it?" the officer above asked.

"Yes we did. I'm going to tie a couple of feet from the end around Cassie."

Antonio shined the light up the chute. "How far do you think it is between floors?"

"I'm guessing around ten to twelve feet."

"Not bad."

"Not bad," Cassie said. "You forgot to add the few feet getting up into the hole. Dear God, I'm not going to be able to do this. I know I can't."

"You have to if you want to survive."

"I've been on investigative cases where my life was in jeopardy if I made the wrong move or wasn't able to hold my breath. But this is a whole different story. I am so scared. I don't think I will be able to do this. That's why I think you should go up there first."

Antonio shook his head side to side. "Nope. You are first." Taking the rope, he tied it tightly around her waist. He pulled on the slack. "Feels like it is secure above. Are you ready up there?"

"Yes we are."

He turned to Cassie. "I know you're scared. But you have to trust me on this. Just hold onto the rope."

Cassie leaned into him and kissed his lips. "Okay, I'm ready."

Antonio leaned down, pushed his head between her legs and lifted her up onto his shoulders.

Cassie guided her head into the opening. Immediately she sneezed, seven times in a row before they stopped.

"Okay," she yelled up. "I'm ready."

A light shined down the chute. "I can see you," the officer said.

"And I can see spider webs, dust and weird bugs," she complained.

"Don't look," Antonio said from below her.

"I can't help but look. It's giving me the creeps. I don't think I'm going to make it out of here alive."

"Baby, hold onto the rope. Try to pull yourself up."

"I couldn't even do that in gym. I also fought with the gym teacher about the rope session of the class," her voice cracked.

"I know, baby. But you have to do this. I know you can."

"Don't be scared," the officer's voice echoed down the opening. "What's your name?"

"Cassie."

"Hi Cassie, I'm Vic. I know this is hard for you."

"Yes it is. All I see is a light shining down at me with spider webs and dead bugs caught in the webs staring me in the face." Goose bumps appeared on her bare arms. She wouldn't have been so grossed out if she had long sleeves on. But with the temperatures being close to sixty-five earlier, there was no need to wear anything else.

"I'm going to set the stage for you. But you have to work with me on this," Vic said.

"Okay," Cassie said in a whisper. "I'm just scared. How long is this going to take to do?"

"If you listen to me, not long. All I need from you is to concentrate on coming up to meet me."

"Okay, Vic," she called up the hole. "Love you," she said to Antonio before taking hold of the rope.

"Listen to everything I tell you. I want you to start by standing on the knot of the rope."

Antonio shined the flashlight on the knot. "It's okay. Vic is trained in rescue. He will guide you. Listen to everything he tells you. There is no room for panic." He tapped her ass. "I'll be up right behind you."

Cassie took a deep breath. Looking up the dark hole, she said, "Okay Vic. I'm ready. The sooner I come up, the sooner Antonio will be up there with me."

"Good girl. Now close your eyes. Think of yourself in a sailboat in the middle of the Caribbean. The water is blue, the sky doesn't have a cloud to be found with the scent of coconut in the air."

"That sounds nice," Cassie said, not opening her eyes.

"Hold onto the rope with your right hand, reach your left hand up as high as you can go, use your knees to secure the rope between your legs. Let me know when you do that."

Cassie reached with her left hand. "Okay. I did that."

"Great. Now hold onto the rope with your left hand, with your right hand reach up as high as you can."

"Okay, that wasn't so bad."

"I want you to keep repeating the process. And each time you change hands, I want you to pull yourself up as much as you can. I'm on the other end, trying my best to help pull you up."

"Okay." Keeping her eyes closed, Cassie continued the pattern, concentrating on the blue water. This had turned into a do or die situation. Damn, her life had just begun. She was finally happy.

"You're almost here," Vic said.

"Oh God. My friends. I wonder if my friends are okay." As soon as she spoke, she slid back down another foot.

"Focus, Cassie. You are almost up here. I need your help to complete this task."

"Okay. Sorry. I came off the sailboat."

"Get back on. Stay with me."

Cassie didn't answer. Instead she kept repeating the process. She kept her eyes closed focusing on crystal clear water. When she felt something against her shoulder, she let out a scream. But instead of falling back down, she felt herself being pulled up from under her arms, then placed her onto her back. She tried to speak, but the words wouldn't come out.

Slowly opening her eyes, she looked around the candlelit room. "Antonio," she called out in a breathless voice.

"Antonio will be with you in a few minutes. How are you feeling?"

"I don't know. Your voice. You're Vic."

"Yes I am."

"If it weren't for you, I'd still be down there. Thank you."

Vic extended his hand to her. "Let me help you up."

Cassie raised her arm. But instead of taking Vic's hand, her hand fell into Antonio's.

"You're here." Cassie threw her arms around Antonio's neck.

"Where else would I be," he said, hugging her tightly. "I'm so glad you are okay. But now," he dropped his arms and stepped back, "I have to find out what's going on."

"Slow down," Vic said. "Right now there isn't much we can do. The station is flooded out downstairs. Troy and Crystal, the new civilian, are down the hall in the storage closet looking to see if there is any emergency gear we can use."

"I remember at one time we had stored the gear in there, but I can't be sure."

Vic held up his hand. "Not to worry. You stay here with your lady friend. I'll go take Harris with me and see what Troy and Crystal are doing."

"Yell if you need me."

Cassie stood shivering. The rain had just about ended, but the dampness in the air made her feel cold. Antonio took a navy blue police sweat shirt hoodie off the hook by the door and slid it over her head.

"This should keep you warm."

"Thank you," she whispered.

Antonio walked over to the window. When she heard him gasp, she joined him. Across the canal, downtown Manhattan was black. They had lost their lights too. The street was covered in water. Down the other way she saw a boat with two people, with one of them holding a big flashlight looking around.

"This is devastating. I have never seen Richmond Terrace look like this before. Sure it has flooded out, but not to the extreme where a boat is the only way out."

"Are we going to get out of here?" she asked, taking hold of his arm.

"Yes." Antonio lifted her chin until their eyes met. "I promise you, we will get out of here."

"I hope—"

"Antonio."

They both turned around as Crystal walked toward them with a blanket.

"We found a whole bunch of supplies in the storage room down the hall."

"Awesome," Antonio said. "Thank God our previous captain was a hoarder."

"Hoarder isn't the word. He saved everything down to the previous captain's nameplate." Crystal placed the blanket around Cassie's shoulders. "Vic needs your help. I'll stay here with Cassie."

Cassie turned to face Antonio. "Go. I'll be fine."

Antonio kissed her forehead. "I want the two of you to stay put. No walking around the building. We'll have to find out how much damage there is to the building, and how we're going to get out."

"Please don't be long."

"Promise."

Before Cassie had time to say anything to Crystal, they heard a big bang, which caused them to run into the hall. But it turned out to be too late. The floor in the room the men were in had collapsed.

"Oh my God," her voice echoed down the hall. "Antonio."

Within seconds, Vic, Harris and Antonio popped their heads out from the room next to it.

"What happened?" Antonio said.

Cassie pointed to the storage room before collapsing onto the floor.

* * * *

Sophia made the decision to go over the table. The water looked disgusting. Shining her flashlight down, pieces of food, broken dishes and silverware lined the floor. On the other side of the table sat a piece of wood. Repositioning the flashlight, she'd swear the wood looked like a board from the boardwalk. She shook her head. Impossible.

This was a do or die situation. She was scared shitless of climbing over the table. However, the way the table got stuck, if she held onto the top, she might make it to the other side. She just wished she wasn't so scared. She hated the ocean, was frightened of it.

Okay, I can do this.

Sophia put one foot up on the table. With her left hand, she grabbed onto the top edge of the table as leverage. After finding her balance, she shined the flashlight ahead. As she walked along the table, she stepped on something that pinched her. She let out a scream, lost her footing, and fell into the water. Even though the water was shallow, she couldn't get herself up. In a state of panic, she tried to stand but kept sliding off the table, which blocked the passageway. *I can do this. I have to just open my eyes, try my best to see where I am going.*

Sophia reached her arms out above her head, and then brought them down to her side. She repeated this process a few times before trying again. This time when she put her feet down, they touched the floor and she stood up. Turning her head side to side, she sighed in relief. But in the process she lost her flashlight. Now she stood in complete darkness except for the slight shadow of the moon breaking through the clouds.

Reaching her hands out in front of her, she made her way down the long hallway feeling her way. Whatever she stepped on crunched beneath her feet. She didn't look down. She didn't want to know. This nightmare just seemed to keep getting worse. Again, she tripped, falling into the water. The rawness of the night sent chills throughout her body. The exit out of there was only feet away, but the amount of rubbish on the floor was horrific, making the path almost impossible to escape. Coming from the back of the building, she could still hear the waves crashing against the boardwalk.

The worst part was being here alone. In the distance she still heard sirens and the echo of people screaming or crying.

She had to get to the doorway leading her out of here. Her eyes had adjusted to the dark, making things a little bit better. Taking small steps, she made her way within feet of the exit, before she fell again. This time when she landed on her left arm, she yelled out in pain as something stabbed her. Looking at her arm, she could see the fork marks. She needed to focus to get herself out of here in one piece.

Sophia was surprised Scott hadn't come looking for her. By now he should have been back from Allentown with his belongings. She'd have to worry about him later. Right now, her main concern would be her journey to the open door, which apparently had been ripped from the hinges, just like the back doors.

Once she made it to the door, she sighed. All she had to do now was get into her car and go home to a long hot bath. But when she walked out onto the deck she was in for the shock of her life. Father Capodanno was no longer a street. It had turned into a river. In the parking lot below, the cars were no longer in spots. Her car sat on its side against the cement electrical box by the curb. The house across the street had the whole side ripped off. On the second floor, a bed hung out of a bedroom, on the verge of falling.

The water stopped inches away from the top of the street sign. No doubt the water had to be at least six feet deep. She spotted a boat drifting down the street.

"Over here," she started yelling, waving her hands.

The boat kept on going, the person in there, not even turning to look her way.

"Help, please come back." Sophia jumped up and down. "Please will someone help me?"

What seemed like hours, but was only ten minutes, before another boat came down the street. This time the boat had a big spotlight shining from the front. Sophia started screaming for help at the top of her lungs. As much as her throat hurt, she knew she had to keep on yelling if she was going to be saved.

When the light turned her way, she screamed again, waving her arms. This time the light blinked on and off.

"I'm here. Please help me."

"I see you," a voice echoed over a megaphone. "I'm coming to get you."

Sophia watched as the boat made its way through the debris. It stopped feet from her, staying afloat.

"Thank you."

"What are you doing here?" asked the elderly fireman.

"I was working. Got stuck in the storm."

The fireman picked up his radio. "Another one who didn't listen to evacuation warnings."

"I didn't hear them."

"Lady, it has been all over the radio and television for days. But no sense in dwelling on that."

"Well, thank you. And again, I had no idea. I don't watch television, let alone open up a newspaper."

"I hope you learned your lesson on the importance of at least watching the news once a day."

"Believe me, I learned my lesson." Sophia looked around. "How am I going to get to you?"

"I'm going to throw you the safety rope." He threw the rope with a hook on its end. "I need for you to wrap the rope around the railing, and then clip it."

Sophia picked up the rope before doing as he said. "Okay. Now you can come get me."

"Miss, you got this all wrong. Since you aren't injured, you are going to have to make your way down to me. That's why I sent you the safety line."

"What do I have to do?" Sophia called out to him.

"You need to use the rope as your guide to the boat. The water is pretty deep, so you must hold onto the rope. Can you swim?" he yelled above the sound of sirens.

"No. As long as my feet don't touch the floor, I can't swim."

"It's okay. Unfortunately, you are at the high point of the water. The water is starting to recede down further, enough for the fire engines to get down there."

"I'm scared."

"I know you are. But you have to listen to everything I say to you. I'm just as afraid as you. I've been on the job for over seventeen years. Never once did I have to do a water rescue. You have to work with me on this. Okay?"

Sophia nodded her head. "I'm good. Just tell me what I have to do."

"I want you to hold onto the rope. You'll need to use it as your lifeline to the boat."

"I don't think I can do this," Sophia cried. "I'm so cold. What if the rope breaks from the railing while I'm on my way to you?"

"I will pull you in. You cannot let go of the rope. Do you understand?"

"Yes."

"I promise if you follow my instructions, I will have you at a safe location, in dry clothes, within the hour. But you must listen, trust me."

"Okay. I'm ready."

Sophia took hold of the rope. The twine felt coarse against her soft skin. Taking a deep breath, she stood at the opening of the deck.

"Sit down on the edge. Hold on tightly to the rope. Slowly slide off the edge and use the rope to guide you to the boat," he explained.

"Okay. Here we go."

The moment Sophia slid off the edge, her body slammed into water much colder than what it was inside. Sophia kept her eyes on the boat. The light the fireman had shining was bright enough for her to see the debris floating around her. Tears rose in her eyes as her panic swelled.

"Miss, you have to focus. I know this is scary, but you're almost here."

"One of the boardwalk workers is dead. I saw him floating inside. I couldn't have helped him. The wave was so high. When it crashed into the building, we got swept away."

"You need to concentrate on me. Getting here."

"There's so much water. I never go into the ocean. But now, it's like the ocean has come to get me."

"You're talking in riddles."

"The rope. It's hurting my hands. I can't hold on anymore."

Sophia let go. Slowly, her body descended. She closed her eyes. This had been her dream years ago. So many times she tried to end her life, but just couldn't. If this had happened a year ago, she would have opened her mouth and welcomed the tranquil state she always wondered about. But now, her life had turned around. She was back home with her friends and met a man who sent shivers up and down her spine.

As soon as her feet touched the ground she pushed herself up. Using her arms, she did the doggy paddle until her head came out of the water. She took a deep breath, reached for the round life preserver, which had been attached to another rope. The fireman pulled on the rope bringing her up to the boat.

"Are you all right?" he asked, placing a blanket around her.

"Yes," she whispered. "Thank you. Mister…"

"Hank. You can call me Hank."

"I'm Sophia."

"I don't know what you were doing out tonight, but I'm going to do my best to get you to the shelter."

He pulled on the string and the small motor moved the boat forward. They rode down Father Capodanno until they were in shallow water. Immediately, another fireman walked to the boat in his rubber pants to meet them. She stepped over the edge and into knee-deep water. The fireman led her down the street to a large concrete building. She had to pass through these streets thousands of times never noticing this building, which was set back from the curb.

Sophia walked into a candlelit room. There were people everywhere, along with cots all lined up.

"Hi," a short red headed elderly lady greeted her. "Come with me. We'll get some attention for your arm first, then find you a place to rest."

Luckily, the doctor helping out only used two stitches to close the wound on her forearm. After telling her to get a tetanus shot when she got the stitches out in seven to ten days and to keep the bandage clean, he let her go. Sweat pants and a T-shirt sat on the cot the woman led her to. Sophia changed before lying down. Tonight's disaster turned into a miracle.

She'd just close her eyes for only a couple of minutes before she tried to get in touch with Scott and Madison.

Chapter Nine

The night was long. Madison barely slept. Every time she dozed off, she'd hear a noise, waking her immediately. At one point, Dino covered her with all the blankets, holding her snuggly in his arms. Now the sound of foghorns woke her. This time the sun shined through the tiny vent in the ceiling.

Dino lay fast asleep snoring. She knew he'd stayed up all night making sure nothing happened to her. Slowly she slid out of his arms without waking him. She had to go downstairs to assess the damage.

With Dino next to her she felt safe, but now their future remained uncertain. Yes, everything below them consisted of material things, but the memories attached to them could never be recaptured.

Quietly, she crawled to the stairs. When they creaked open, she looked over her shoulder to Dino who didn't flinch. She made her way down carefully and cringed stepping on the wet rug at the bottom. To think they just put in this rug a few years ago. As she headed down the hall, water splashed under her feet, up her legs. Reaching her bedroom, she was grateful to see their wedding picture and the picture with the girls remained unmarred.

She lifted the house phone to no dial tone, and then proceeded to try her cell phone. She dialed Shari's number only to be told all circuits were busy. After a few attempts she quit. There were only two lines left on the battery. She had to save the power, and try later.

Opening the blinds, she looked out and gasped. The streets were inundated. Water was up to people's knees as they walked around furniture and appliances were scattered in the streets, while papers floated on top. All the cars were out of their spaces, scattered all over.

Madison opened the top drawer of her dresser and took out the small white leather jewelry box. Inside sat her cross necklace, the one Dino had bought her over twelve years ago. She placed the long gold chain around her neck. The box also contained Dino's diamond cross and gold wedding band. Opening the chain, she slid his wedding band on it and placed that chain over the other one around her neck too. Before closing the box, she slid on her diamond engagement ring and wedding band. That's all she cared about. Everything else could be replaced. But she couldn't help but peek into her closet. Everything three feet and over had been saved, the rest of their things had been under water.

Now the hardest part would be going downstairs. Last night the water had reached the second floor. Hopefully it receded down there too.

Madison walked down the stairs to see sunlight lit the living room. Strange. She had the blinds closed. The water was knee high. Beautiful sunbeams came in through the blown out front window. As she walked through the room, she kept her eyes down on the floor careful of all the broken glass. She didn't need a shard in her foot.

In the kitchen, the sliding glass door frame lay broken against the island with the glass scattered all over the place. The water seemed an inch or two lower in the kitchen. But on further investigation, as quickly as the water flowed out the sliding glass doors was as fast as it spiraled back in. She picked up the kitchen chairs off the floor and pushed them in under the table. Hopefully later they would be able to sit down to have a normal dinner. Who was she kidding? So far, the way the house looked, she wouldn't be doing any cooking for a very long time.

Out of curiosity, she looked into the kitchen cabinet. The soup dishes and coffee mugs that remained on the shelves were filled with water. Most of the dinner plates were broken on the floor. Reaching on top of the refrigerator, she closed her eyes as her hand touched the platter. With a deep breath, she stretched out her other hand to bring it down. She opened her eyes. Relieved, she smiled. The seventy-five year old platter that belonged to her grandmother didn't have a single chip. Madison returned her treasure to the top of the refrigerator.

Drawing in another deep breath, her next stop would be Dino's studio. But instead, she walked out the open doorway that used to be sliding glass doors. Stepping down, her bare feet touched the saturated dirt. Water circled around her calves, a big difference from last night when the whole first floor of their house was covered with it. She would wait a while before she attempted walking over to Shari's house. She had to make sure her best friend was okay. Shari only lived a mile and a half away. If she took her time, she would be able to get through the flooded streets.

Standing outside Dino's studio, she knew everything had been ruined without even looking. The hardest part would be confirming his fears. This studio had been his whole life. Everything he worked hard for.

Again, the backdoor of the studio had been blown out. The first thing she saw was his file cabinet on its side. The drawers were on the floor with all the paper contents floating around the room. Madison covered her face with her hands and cried. Everything had been destroyed—his equipment, his computer, amplifiers and especially his black baby grand piano, the one he had been teaching her how to play.

"It's okay," Dino said, wrapping his arms around her from behind. "Everything can be replaced."

"This is your life." She pointed, leaning her head against his shoulder.

"This room is filled with material things. Sure they are costly, but without you everything in this room would have been meaningless."

"I know. But all the hard work you have done is all gone."

Dino dropped his arms. He walked around the room before turning to face her. "I have a copy of everything I have ever done on a thumb drive, or should I say multiple thumb drives. You can never rely on a computer. It could crash at any given time for no reason at all."

"Are you kidding me?" she asked, her eyes bulging wide open.

"Nope. I learned that from you."

"You did?"

Dino leaned over, reaching for the tambourine. "Do you remember when we were going through the mounds of papers in the corner of this room before I moved my studio from the city to here?"

"Yes. They were copies of my manuscripts for my three book series."

"Exactly. You're the one who emphasized to me that you can't trust computers. You had a hard copy of everything you have done, a thumb drive, plus an external hard drive. You know what, I took your advice."

"Where did you store them? Everything down here is destroyed."

Dino walked across the room to the closet in the corner. As he opened the door, he jumped back when the door fell off its hinges. "Wow, close call."

"I know. We have to be very careful. There's nowhere to go unless we go out on foot. Our cars are destroyed along with our neighbors'."

"Say a prayer this waterproof safe is really waterproof."

"Oh dear God, I hope so."

Dino placed the safe on his desk. Before he opened it, he stood in silence, looking at his monitor and mixing boards. Her heart went out for him. She had talked him into moving his business to their home. At the suggestion, Dino couldn't have been happier. The rent for his studio in Manhattan had gone up forty-five percent. Right before he moved his business, he had been losing money.

Within a month, he had an extension put on the back of the house, soundproofing all the walls so he didn't disturb the neighbors while he worked into the wee hours of the morning.

After doing the sign of the cross, he slid open his desk drawer and took out a musical note key chain. He slid the key into the lock. He turned it until they heard the click. Slowly he lifted the cover.

Turning to Madison, he grinned. "Bone dry, baby. Come on, feel it. Bone dry," he repeated again raising his fist in triumph.

"That's wonderful." Madison threw her arms around his neck. "We have a long road ahead of us. I don't know if our lives will ever be the same."

"As long as we have each other, our lives will remain the same." Tears escaped from Dino's eyes. "Yes, this studio is my life. But the thought of losing you gets me choked up. I love you so much. I could never live without you."

"I love you more." She slid her arms around his neck. "We will rebuild together."

"Another possibility is starting over in a new house. But," he held his hand up, "that's a decision for the both of us to make at a later date. We need to figure out what the hell we are going to do, where we are going to stay. Right now we have no utilities or bed to sleep in."

"That's why I'm going to take a walk over to Shari's. The circuits are all busy on the cell phones, the landlines are all down."

"I don't feel comfortable with you walking there by yourself."

"We have no other choice. Someone has to stay here to guard all our possessions, or should I say what's left of them."

"Whatever I tell you, you are going to go anyway. But I can assure you one thing. I'm not letting you go alone. Nothing here is worth watching over if I don't have you."

Dino took her in his arms.

"I am so scared."

"Me too."

* * * *

Shari woke up to the sound of Thomas's cries. Within minutes, he jumped up on her bed. Sitting up, she went to throw her legs onto the floor and screamed out in pain when she tried to move her left leg.

"Mommy, are you all right?"

"Yes, Thomas. I am." How could she tell him the pain was unbearable, as her tears threatened to turn into full-fledged hysteria? She couldn't channel into Madison, which wasn't a good thing. Between her mind being fogged and Thomas crying, she felt like her head was ready to explode.

Tommy walked into the bedroom with a dish of sliced banana. "Hey, my two favorite people in the whole wide world. I sliced fruit for the two of you. While you two eat, I'm going to go out, see what's going on, see if I can get you to the hospital. Your leg needs to be looked at."

"Yes, it does. I think it's broken. The pain is affecting my ability to channel into my friends. I don't know if they are okay. I can't go out to check on them. Can you do that for me?"

"What's channeling, Mommy?"

"It's when Mommy knows what Aunt Madison is doing."

"Is Aunt Madison coming to visit us?" he asked, taking a piece of sliced banana off the tray.

Tommy kissed the top of Thomas and Shari's head. "I will check on Madison after I check out the roads. I don't know if I'm going to be able to get through. I'll be back as soon as I can."

"Be careful."

"I'll stay with her," Heather said, standing in the doorway.

"Thank you. Make sure she doesn't try to get off the bed until I get back." He turned to Shari. "Do you need to use the bathroom before I leave?"

"No, I'm good."

"See you in a bit."

Heather sat down on the bed cross-legged. "Aunt Shari, I am really nervous about my mother. Do you think she is all right?"

"I'm sure she is. The last time I spoke to her, she was waiting for the plane to come home."

Shari closed her eyes and drifted off.

Fay is pacing in front of a huge glass window. In the distance sat an airplane. An announcement over the loudspeaker in a heavy British accent sends Fay to a large lit board. Fay points up at the board and starts cheering when she sees her flight is leaving. "I need to get home to my baby," she keeps mumbling under her breath as she drags her big piece of carry-on luggage along with her.

Fay taps on her cell phone again in hopes of getting in touch with Heather. When the call doesn't go through, she continues by calling all her friends, hoping someone would answer. Frustrated by the clogged up circuits, she drops her phone back into her handbag as she rushes to the entrance gate.

Shari reached for her head. Between the pain in her leg and her pounding head, she needed to go back to sleep.

"Are you okay?" Heather asked.

"Yes. Your mother is fine. Her plane is getting ready to leave. She is so worried about you. I'm guessing none of us have cell phone service. The storm probably knocked down the towers in the area. But I did see her trying to get in contact with all of us."

"That's great. I can't wait for Mom to come home. I know she's very forgetful, but she needs to be here, see what's going on. I just don't know what to do about the store."

"I know. I was going to suggest we all went over there today to clean up, see what could be salvaged. How stupid of me not to listen to all the warnings."

"Don't beat yourself. None of us listened."

"I'm going to need your help." Shari pointed to her leg. "Since I am immobile, I'm going to need you to snoop around, see what's going on."

"Oh no." Heather waved her finger. "I promised Uncle Tommy I would take care of you and Thomas. But I'll make you a deal."

"A deal? What do you think this is a game show?" Shari joked, not wanting Heather to know how scared she was.

Heather shook her head, her eyes moving from side to side. "No."

"Forget it." Shari waved her off. "It's a joke. Tell me, what do you have in mind?"

"Let me make breakfast for the two of you. After replacing the ice on your leg, I'll get Thomas settled here with you before I go check things outside."

"Thank you. I have to get in touch with Madison. I feel she needs me."

"Let me get breakfast going." Heather stood and walked to the door. "The sooner you guys eat, the faster I can go out investigating. Come on Thomas, come help me make Mommy breakfast."

"I butter the toast?"

"Yes you do."

Shari laughed as their voices echoed from the kitchen. Again she tried to move her leg, but instead pain radiated through her whole body. Lifting her phone, she tried Madison again. This time the phone rang, going straight to voice mail. Strange for Madison. She never shut her phone off because she didn't want to miss a phone call.

"Up here," Shari heard Tommy yelling.

"Daddy's home," Thomas's squeaky voice echoed.

Tommy came into her room with another man who she recognized as one of her neighbors.

"You won't believe what it's like outside. But before I get into that, I ran into Eric."

"You live down behind the deli."

"Yes." Eric had an old-fashioned black doctor's bag he put down on the bed. "Tommy told me you were having pain in your left leg."

"Oh yes. I think I either sprained it very bad or broke it."

"What does the pain feel like?"

"Pain. I can't move my leg without seeing stars," Shari explained.

"I need to examine your leg."

Shari's eyes popped wide open. "You're going to move it?"

"If I'm going to examine it."

"I got you, baby." Tommy sat down on the bed next to her holding her hand.

"Mommy, are you okay?" Thomas asked running by her side.

"Mommy's okay. Did you finish making breakfast with Heather?"

"No."

"Go tell Heather we need another four slices of toast."

"Gotcha," Thomas said running out of the room.

Shari took a deep breath. "Okay, I am ready."

Eric pressed on her leg. Shari screamed out in pain, squeezing Tommy's hand.

"Sorry," Eric said. "I know this hurts, but I need to find where the break is."

"Her leg is broken?" Tommy asked.

"I'm pretty sure it's broken at the ankle. It's hard to see because her leg is so swollen, but if you look here," he pointed to her ankle, "you can see where the bone is sticking out."

"Can you fix it?" Shari asked.

"Unfortunately, no. I can recommend you to an orthopedic doctor who can set it for you, but you need to go to the hospital."

"Can you be there with me and Tommy?"

"I can stop by while I'm on my rounds up in maternity."

"Maternity?"

"Yes. I'm an OB/GYN."

"And you know about bones?"

Eric chuckled. He withdrew a syringe, filled it with liquid from a small brown bottle, then inserted the needle into her arm. "This should help you with the pain."

"Thank you, Eric."

Eric nodded. "Tommy, call for an ambulance while I wrap her leg."

"What's going on outside?" Shari asked when Tommy walked out of the room.

"A disaster. I have never seen so much water in my life. I tried to get out with my car this morning to go down to the hospital, but I couldn't get through. A few blocks from here there is so much water the fire department is rescuing people by boat."

"Oh my God."

"You can sure as hell say that," Tommy said standing in the doorway. "Apparently, the hospital is closed. The first two floors are under water. An ambulance is coming from Brooklyn."

"Where are they taking me?"

"To the hospital right over the bridge."

"I don't want to go there."

"You have no other choice. The whole waterfront of Staten Island is under water along with a greater part of Hylan Boulevard."

"He's right," Eric said. "Besides everything being flooded out, it is imperative your leg is set, then put in a cast to prevent any other damage."

"You're right. Where I go doesn't matter. All they're going to do is set my leg and send me home. When are they coming?"

"They're not sure," Tommy said.

"That's just great."

"What's the difference, we can't go anywhere. Just lay there and relax."

"That's the best advice anyone can give you," Eric said. "The painkiller should start taking effect very soon. I'm going to head back out. I want to check in on a few of our elderly neighbors to make sure they are okay."

"Thank you, Eric."

"I'll check back on you later."

Tommy slid off the bed. He extended his hand out to Eric. "Thanks again for your help. Imagine it takes a tragedy to get to know your neighbors."

"That's the way it always happens."

"I'll be right back. Let me walk Eric to the door. Do you need anything?"

"I would love a cup of coffee."

"So would I."

* * * *

Fay opened her eyes and looked out the tiny airplane window. Tears sprang immediately to her eyes as she recognized the tip of Long Island. All she saw were houses surrounded by water. At one part, it looked like Long Island had been cut in half with the ocean overrunning directly into the bay.

Her heart pounded when the plane passed over the Rockaways. The boardwalk had been washed out to sea. The train tracks were also washed away, the streets full of water. This had to be some sort of nightmare. The British meteorologist said there was a storm, but never in her dreams did she ever think there would be this much damage.

Within minutes, the plane traveled over Coney Island. This time her tears turned into sobbing. The ocean had taken over the beach with no sand to be found. All she saw was the very top of the fishing pier as well as the gazebo. This couldn't be. And then they were over Staten Island. Her sobs turned into hysteria, causing the passengers around her to look her way.

"Look." She pointed out the window. "Everything is gone. The beach is gone in Staten Island. There's water all over the place. Father Capodanno is under water. The streets are wiped out. Oh my God," she cried covering her face with her hands.

"Heather," she mumbled. Reaching into her handbag she took a hold of her rosary beads and held them close to her heart. This couldn't be happening. Her baby was somewhere out there. She had no way of knowing if Heather was okay.

How the hell would she get from the airport to her house? She hadn't taken notice to see if the Verrazano Bridge had opened. What if the Outerbridge Crossing, the Bayonne or the Goethals Bridge were closed? How would she be able to make it into the island? If she had to, she'd walk over the Bayonne Bridge. But all her worries were put to ease when they passed over the Goethals Bridge. She spotted cars driving across.

She was only two hours away from being home. Once she knew Heather was okay, she would check on Madison, Shari, Cassie and Sophia. The last thing to do would be to assess the damage at her store.

If she learned anything from her trip to Italy, she learned that family is one of the most important things in her life. Plus after her visit to the Vatican, she renewed her faith in God. She'd say the rosary, which always left her with the feeling of peace.

Chapter Ten

Cassie opened her eyes to see Antonio staring down at her. The last thing she had remembered was hearing a noise, which led to a room collapsing, scaring her tremendously.

"What happened?" she asked, pulling up the heavy blanket to her neck.

"You passed out from exhaustion. We had a pretty rough night here, but we made it through."

"Thank God." Cassie pointed to the blanket. "Where did this come from?"

"We found a few in the supply room. I'm sure it isn't the cleanest, but it was heavy enough to get us through the cold night. I just wish I would have found you dry clothes."

"I think that's the least of our problems."

"I waited for you to wake up before I went with the others."

"Where are you going?"

"We need to check out the rest of the building. See if there is a way to get out of here. God only knows how much water there is through this building. At least for now, we are safe."

Antonio reached both his hands down to her. Cassie took them and stood up. "You're not going to leave me alone?" she asked tightening her grip on his hands.

"I wouldn't do that. Crystal will stay with you while I go with Harris and Vic."

"The guys are waiting for you," Crystal said, walking in. "After taking a quick look around, things don't look very promising."

"What do you mean?" Cassie asked.

"LoParlo is dead," Vic said.

"Are you kidding?" Antonio asked, pivoting around on the heels of his shoes.

"He drowned. He probably couldn't get out of the building."

"I knew I should have taken a quick walk around the floor, or just yelled out seeing if anyone needed help." Antonio slapped his forehead.

"His death isn't your fault. You saved Cassie's life. You are damn lucky to be alive."

"But he has a wife and three kids under the age of seven."

"Antonio, I feel the same grief you feel. However, we need to focus on the moment. It's now up to the three of us to get Cassie and Crystal the hell out of here. But first we need to find a safe passageway," Vic said, walking to the door. "Harris is waiting for us down the hall."

"I'll be right back." Antonio kissed her forehead. "I want you and Crystal to stay in this room. You are safe here. Okay?"

Cassie nodded her head. "Be careful."

"I have to be. We have to get out of here. I want to see my kids, make sure they are okay, and get you back home where we can try to get things back to normal." Antonio blew her a kiss from the doorway. "I want to spend more time with you. See you in a bit."

When Antonio left, she looked over at Crystal who stood with her arms folded looking out the window. Joining her, Cassie gasped. There were rowboats and canoes floating down the streets filled with people. A chill ran through Cassie causing her body to shake uncontrollably.

"Hey, everything is going to be okay," Crystal said, tucking the long strand of dirty blonde hair back into her ponytail. "Today the water level is much lower than yesterday."

"How do you know that? To me, Richmond Terrace still looks the same as last night."

"Yes it does. But look," she pointed straight out, "this morning we can see the top of the metal gate. And look over there," she pointed to her left, "the water level is no longer covering the cars."

"Are you sure?" Cassie asked not remembering much about last night.

"Yes. I promise you things are different. I totally remember. I couldn't sleep, so I stood here by the window most of the night trying to figure out a way out of here. With these big padlocks on the windows, and with no one knowing where the key is, I wondered if we'd ever get out of here if the water level rose any higher."

"I'm so sorry I slept through it all. If I would have known you were up, I would have kept you company."

"No sense for the two of us to be up worrying. Between you and me," she whispered, "Antonio is some hell of a catch. All the ladies go after him. Boy, were they in for a letdown when he started bringing you around here."

"I got that feeling every time I walked into the precinct. I thought my ego was playing games with me, so I never said anything."

Crystal shook her head, smirking. "No, it wasn't you. Antonio is really charming. But I'm glad to see he found himself a nice woman."

"I'm scared."

"Yeah, me too. But the guys are trained for situations like this. Look how Antonio and Vic got you up here. I can assure you when they get us out of here they will get another medal of accommodation."

"I hope you're right. Looking out there," Cassie pointed straight ahead, "seems like something out of the movies. Not something that happens here in Staten Island."

"I agree with you. I just wish we could get out of here. I want to go home."

Cassie heard the panic in her voice. Crystal shared her fear. This situation wasn't something she had prepared for at all. Hearing footsteps above them, they both looked up at the ceiling.

"What's that noise?"

"Not sure. But I do wonder where the men went. I hope they didn't forget about us," Crystal mumbled.

Her wet shoes squished as she turned toward the door when she heard footsteps coming toward them. "Come on," she said. "That has to be the guys."

Standing in the doorway, she saw Antonio and Vic walking down the hall.

"Are you girls okay?" Antonio asked.

"Yes, we are," Crystal answered for them. "Where's Harris?"

Antonio and Vic looked at each other, neither speaking a word. They didn't have to. By the look on their faces Cassie already knew what had happened.

"He tried to get the life preservers on the other side of the room that had collapsed," Antonio said, not making eye contact with them.

"That storage room has been off limits for years. Major repairs on the beam were to take place sometime next month," Vic explained.

"We begged him not to go in there. We had already found two in the other room, but he insisted we try for another one because Vic doesn't swim."

Crystal covered her face with her hands. "Oh dear God." And then she fell to her knees and broke down.

"No, you can't do this," Cassie said. "Everything will be okay."

"I never will be." Crystal looked up at Cassie, her eyes full of tears. "Harris is my boyfriend. We kept our relationship quiet, to not cause any problems."

Cassie knelt next to her. "I'm so sorry."

"Yeah, so am I," both Antonio and Vic said at the same time, then Antonio continued, "But we can't stay here. You ladies have to hold it together if we're going to get out of here."

"Where is he?"

Antonio bit his bottom lip, and put his head down. "He fell through the floor face first into the water. The concrete floor fell on top of him. We tried to help him, but we were too late."

"I'm sorry, Crystal. Harris was my pal, my partner for years. I can assure you he loved you very much. Never doubt that."

Crystal wiped the tears from her eyes with the back of her hand, stood and reached out to hug Vic. Cassie got to her feet, walked over to Antonio and fell into his arms.

Antonio brushed his big hands through Cassie's hair. "We're going to get out of here. I want to see my kids, start a life with you." He kissed the top of her head before taking a step back. "I know this is tough for all of us, but we have to get going just in case the stairs fill up with water again."

"The staircase is clear down to the first floor," Vic said. "But once we open the door, there is water all over the place. There is a safe area for us to stand on. We tied a rope to the area keeping it safe for the two of you."

"The boat we found up in the storage closet is also attached to the railing. We need to get you girls to safety." Antonio took Cassie's hand and led her to the door down the corridor with Vic and Crystal following behind.

"Once you girls are safe, we need to assist in the rescue mission."

Cassie pulled on Antonio's hand until he turned to face her on the staircase and let the others pass. "You're not coming with me?"

"I can't, babe. Richmond Terrace is a disaster area. People are stuck in their apartments. I promise to keep in touch with you."

"With no cell phone service?"

"Come on. We need to get going. In a few hours high tide will be back in. There are so many people who are trapped."

"Then what are we waiting for," Cassie said, stomping down the stairs. "I don't want to be stuck in here again tonight."

When they joined the others, Antonio slowly opened the door. Some water came in, adding to the four inches already at their feet.

"Where's the boat?" Cassie asked.

Vic pointed. "On the other side of the railing."

"The boat is in the water," Crystal said.

"Yes it is," Vic said. "We need to move fast. There's no time to waste."

Antonio secured the life preservers on them before helping her and Crystal into the boat. Cassie's stomach bubbled. The street and the Narrows had become one. If the boat went the wrong way, they would be floating toward the Atlantic Ocean.

Antonio and Vic used small paddles to push the orange boat toward Bay Street. After sitting quietly for close to fifteen minutes, they came to a stop when the boat hit the asphalt. Within seconds, two firemen were at their sides, helping them, throwing heavy blankets around them.

"Thanks guys." Antonio shook their hands. "Please take care of these ladies. This is my girlfriend," he put his arm around Cassie, "and this is Crystal. She just lost her boyfriend at the precinct. Please make sure they get special care."

"We got them. They will be at the shelter up at the church."

Antonio kissed her. "I'll check in on you later. I don't know when I'll get back to you. Don't forget that I love you."

Before she could answer him or give him a kiss, he pushed the boat back into the water and jumped in with Vic. Cassie stood there holding the blanket around her watching the boat until she didn't see it anymore, not knowing what to expect next.

* * * *

Sophia looked around the room shocked. She couldn't remember anything after changing her clothes. There had to be at least a hundred people surrounding her on their own cots. Kids ran around the room crying, while adults had dazed looks on their faces. Standing, she walked over to a woman who wore a badge around her neck.

"Excuse, me. Can you tell me where the ladies room is?"

"Walk under the basketball hoop, straight through those doors. The bathroom is the forth door on your left."

"Thank you." As she walked down the hall, she took notice of the shine on the green and burgundy floor. Funny how schools were able to keep their floors shiny for over forty years, yet she couldn't keep her kitchen floor polished for anything.

At the sink, she leaned over and splashed water on her face. The cold water felt good, waking her up. Raising her head, she looked into the small round mirror at her reflection. Black streaks lined her face, her hair was frizzy with small pieces of paper and dirt in it. Turning on the other faucet, she stuck her head under and let the water roll through her hair. She proceeded to wash her hair using soap from the nearby dispenser before enjoying rinsing it again with clean water.

Sophia looked back into the mirror. Using her fingers, she combed the knots out of her hair. She had to figure out where she was first, before devising a plan on where to go. No doubt she wouldn't be able to get back into her house, since she lived not far from the ocean. Pushing the door open, she returned back to the gymnasium, looking for the woman who had directed her to the bathroom.

"Excuse me," Sophia yelled above the noise waving her hand.

She made her way through the crowd toward the woman who had gotten lost in the crowd again. Standing in the middle of the room she looked around again. What was going on outside? What had happened? Even better, how did she get here?

Finally, she spotted her cot and sat. Her pillowcase had big yellow polka dots making finding her cot easier. Once there, she didn't see her handbag. Where the hell did she leave it?

"Excuse me," she said to the young girl in the next cot. "Did you see my handbag?"

"No. You came in late last night. You were really out of it. From what I understand, you are lucky to be alive." She coughed. "I'm Anne."

"Sophia." She warmly smiled. "Do you know where we are?"

"You're at the school shelter on Hylan Boulevard."

Sophia leaped off the cot. "We are?"

"Yes." She must have been rescued from close by. "This seems to be the only area in a mile radius that didn't get flooded out or lost electricity."

"Thank you."

202
Karen Cino

Sophia looked back at the cot realizing she had no possessions with her. Not that it mattered. Hurrying, she walked across the gym to the doors leading to outside. That's where she found the lady who she had lost in the crowd.

She held out her hand stopping her. "You can't go out there."

"Why can't I? You can't keep me prisoner here."

"You're right. But I really don't know what is going on out there. If it's safe or not."

"I'm willing to take my chances." Sophia pushed open the metal door. "I have a friend who doesn't live far from here. But I promise you, if it isn't safe, I will come back."

"I don't suggest—"

Sophia ignored the warning. Shari lived only a mile from the school, approximately a fifteen minute walk if she walked fast. However, the fifteen minute walk turned into over an hour. By the time she reached the corner, she gasped in horror. A big colonial home with an octagon room in the front had been pushed off its foundation, the octagon room ripped off the front of the house. She couldn't help but stare. She could see right into the house, the pink and white polka dot comforter, the white furniture and clothes all over the place.

A bigger shock was the cars that had apparently floated right out of their spaces. A few were on their sides, while others were up on lawns.

The next four homes all had the same damage, being torn completely off their foundation, with parts of the house torn to shreds. Not paying attention, she walked into a puddle of water. The further she walked, the deeper the water became. She wanted to turn around when the water reached her knees, but looking ahead, she could see asphalt, so she continued. A few blocks away, the houses were unmarred, a good sign. She worried about Scott and her cat Max. Once she got to Shari's she'd call Scott, make sure he made it back to Staten Island.

Sophia rounded the corner to see the boarded up windows of Shari's shop. The door was locked, so she proceeded to ring the doorbell. When no one answered, she rang the bell again, plus knocked too.

"Coming." She heard Heather yelling.

Heather opened the door. "Are you okay?" she asked, stepping aside.

"Yes, now I am."

"You're all wet. Where are you coming from?"

"From the school down the road. I can use a hot cup of coffee."

"Come on upstairs. I'm sure Aunt Shari has dry clothes for you."

Sophia walked up the stairs with Heather following behind. In the living room, Thomas sat at the cocktail table playing with his blocks.

"How did you get here?" Sophia asked, bending down to pick up the blocks that fell.

"I walked. My house is probably flooded out. I didn't know where else to go."

"Do I hear Sophia?" She heard Shari say from the other room.

Sophia bent down next to Thomas. "Yes, you do."

"You're going to have to come in to me. I am laid up in here with a broken leg."

Sophia stood up and walked down the hall. "What the hell happened to you?" she asked from the doorway, looking at Shari on the bed with her leg wrapped on top of a pillow.

"I was just about to ask you the same question. Is your arm all right? You look like you went through the wash."

"That is an understatement. And this is just a few stitches." Sophia walked into the room and sat on the bed next to her.

"You can't imagine what the streets, let alone houses look like out there. I am lucky to be alive."

"Why do you say that?"

"The waves were coming in fast. They were high. Really high. A wave blew out the glass doors in the reception room, sent me flying across the room." Closing her eyes, she could still see the wave coming toward her. Her body shivered. "I've never been so scared in my life. The wave was huge, higher than the building. Everything happened so fast."

Sophia calmed down as she realized Shari rested a hand on her leg. "Everything is okay. But I know you have questions. Please, help yourself to a hot shower and clothes from my closet. When you're done, go grab yourself the cup of coffee you're dying for, while I get my cards together."

* * * *

Shari waited patiently for Sophia to return. Thomas's voice echoed from the living room, asking Sophia to help him finish the puzzle. She admired her friend for making it through the night.

Lifting her tarot deck, she held them tightly to her chest. The warmth of the cards made her feel good. She worried about Tommy who still hadn't come home. She didn't foresee him being in any danger at all. His warm, loving heart would have him out all day helping people in need.

Sophia walked in with a tray of coffee and chocolate cookies. "I thought you'd like to join me."

"Thanks. But I'd rather be having a beer."

"Want me to get you one?"

Shari placed the tarot cards on the bed, waving her index finger. "I can't. The doctor gave me a shot of painkiller. I don't want to take any chances."

"I don't blame you."

Shari took a sip of her coffee before placing the mug on the nightstand. Lifting the deck of cards, she handed them to Sophia. "I want you to close your eyes, shuffle them. When the deck feels right, place them on the bed. Cut them into three piles with your left hand. Then put them back into one."

Sophia started shuffling the cards.

Shari kept her eyes on Sophia. She could feel the tenseness in Sophia's soul, along with her fear. Sophia continued to shuffle the cards. Every time she stopped, she started again. Finally, when she stopped again, she placed the deck on the bed and did as instructed.

"I'm ready."

"Are you sure?" Shari asked picking up the first card.

"Yes."

"Here we go. In the past position is *The Tower*." Shari placed down the first card. "In the present is *The Moon*, followed by *The Ten of Cups* in the future position."

Sophia sat on the bed across from Shari, crossing her legs, rocking back and forth. "I don't like the look of those cards."

"They're not too bad." Shari looked from card to card. "These cards are all in real time."

"What's that supposed to mean?"

Shari picked up *The Tower* card. "This represents yesterday with the storm. You thought your whole life was falling apart, that you weren't going to make it through the night, but you did. That leads you into *The Moon* card. Right now, you're scared, very scared of what's going on."

Shari closed her eyes.

Scott walked out of a motel in New Jersey. As soon as he heard the bridges were opened, he took off. He worried about Sophia, where is she? Is she all right? Is she stuck

somewhere in the middle of the disaster? He had to get home.
Hopefully the roads aren't flooded out. He needed to be sure
Sophia is okay. Why wasn't she answering her phone? He'd
be home in probably a little over an hour.

Shari rolled her neck in a spiral. The tension she felt had
become so intense that her neck cracked numerous times.

"Are you all right?" Sophia nudged her.

"Yes. So is Scott."

"Thank God he's okay."

"He's worried about you." Shari held up her cell phone.
"Apparently cell phone service is down in Staten Island. He's
trying to get in touch with you."

"My phone is at work. When I got hit by the wave, I
wasn't thinking about going back to my office to get my
handbag."

Shari reached over and touched her hand. "Don't worry.
That nightmare is over. But *The Moon* card," she tapped her
index finger on it, "is how you are feeling right now. Fear has
overtaken you. Your fear is for Scott's safety. You have
nothing to worry about. Scott is fine. When the storm hit he
pulled over to the side of the road and stayed at a motel. The
roads were all closed as well as the bridges. He is on his way
home to you now."

Sophia took a deep breath. "Are you sure?"

"Yes. You have nothing to worry about. He is coming with a car full of clothes and supplies."

"What about Max?" she asked, rocking back.

"Max is fine. Scott is fine." Shari touched her arm. "Don't worry. Because look," she held up *The Ten of Cups* card, "things are going to work out. I see plenty of love and harmony in your life in the upcoming months. Things are going to be different for you. I see a change in residence in the spring."

"That's weird. I have no intentions of moving."

"You will be with Scott. I see a big house with a white wooden swing with a white floral pad rocking on the front porch." Shari picked up the cards and returned them back into the deck.

"Your life will be complete."

"I hope you're right. I need good karma."

"And you will receive it."

Sophia sighed. "I'm concerned about the girls. Have they been in contact?"

"Nope." Shari shook her head, frowning. "Not at all. With all the phones out, I don't know what's going on. The last I spoke to Madison, she was with Dino."

"Cassie met Antonio for dinner yesterday afternoon at the precinct. I hope she is with him."

Shari placed her cards back into the silk scarf. "And Fay is on her way home. Now that the airports have opened, she should be on her way. I hope all this doesn't affect her mental being in any way."

"What a shame her store burned down. We're going to have to help her rebuild."

"Yes, we will. We'll have to all team together. Can you hand me the candles?" Shari asked, pointing to her dresser. "I burned the other ones earlier."

Sophia slid off the bed and handed Shari the candles before lifting her coffee mug off the nightstand. "Do you want a refill?"

"No thanks. I had my share of coffee for the day. Maybe you could grab me a bottle of water."

"Not a problem."

While Sophia went into the kitchen, Shari strategically placed the candles in a circle. As she lit the white pillar candle in the middle she channeled into Madison. She was safe, searching for a safe path. Shari concentrated until her ears popped, meaning Madison had picked up on her vibe.

"Hey, are you all right?" Sophia asked, handing her the bottle of water. "You were staring into space."

"I'm good. Come sit back down." After taking a cool gulp, Shari lifted the box of matches to begin the ritual. Tonight, she added a few other candles.

"I start our ritual by lighting a gold candle, which represents protection. I know you guys are strong enough to take care of yourselves, but I need to be certain my friends are protected from the forces Mother Nature has bestowed upon them. So mote it be."

"So mote it be," Sophia chanted with Shari.

"Here you go." Shari handed her the match. "I want you to light the purple candle."

"What does the purple candle represent?" Sophia asked lighting the match from the white candle, so she could light the purple one.

"Purple represents confidence and wisdom. The reason why I choose this candle is to give my friends the confidence to get through whatever situation they are in. I know Madison and Cassie have the wisdom and smarts to get through anything, but from what you have told me, I fear that as strong as they are, they might have to struggle a bit to get free."

"I fear the same thing."

"The purple candle is lit to guide their way. So mote it be."

"So mote it be," Sophia said again. "Lastly," Shari picked up two matches, "we will light the black candle together."

Shari and Sophia both placed their match together over the white candle. When the orange flame blossomed, they both lit the black candle together.

"We both light this black candle in order to put up a double wall to block the negative energies and thoughts surrounding Madison, Cassie and Fay."

Shari closed her eyes. She saw someone with black suede boots walking around looking for help. But she'd be damned if she knew this person.

"Shari, are you okay?" Sophia asked touching her right foot.

She opened her eyes. "Yes. Sorry, I drifted off." Shari extended her hands. Sophia reached out, dropping hers into them. "Everything will be okay. I promise you. The power of our souls will get them through. So mote it be."

"So mote it be."

Chapter Eleven

After staring outside in silence, preparing herself to face the destruction again, Madison finally stepped out the ruined patio doors. Dino took her hand as they both walked out into knee-deep water. Sometime during the night, as they snuggled in each other's arms, trembling in fear, the water had receded. They headed down the stoned path to the front of the house.

Madison gasped. "*Look*," she stuttered, pointing to his car across the street on their neighbor's lawn.

"Where's yours?" Dino asked looking around. "Oh shit, look babe. Your car is all the way down the block on its side."

"This is a nightmare. What are we going to do? Where are we going to go?"

"Let's walk around, see what's going on."

"Oh wait, before we leave, I'm going to run back into the house to get your medicine."

"No, I don't want you doing that."

"Too bad on you. Just give me few minutes to go up in the attic crawl space to get your medicine." Madison gave him a peck on his lips before returning back into the house.

Her heart pounded as she walked around looking at all the damage. Even though they had insurance, the memories could never be replaced. Before going up into the crawl space, she stopped by their bedroom. She took the special heart necklace Dino had given her from the pants she wore the other day and placed it around her neck. Next she took his backpack out of the closet and threw in a change of clothes along with two dry pairs of sneakers. She slid the backpack over her shoulders, walked up the steep wood steps and grabbed the bag with his pills and their other jewelry.

The last thing she took were her grandmother's rosary beads, which were strung around the crucifix over her bed. She placed those around her neck as well before returning outside.

"What took you so long?" Dino asked.

Madison turned to show him the backpack. "I packed us a change of clothes and another pair of sneakers."

"Smart thinking."

"I'm so scared. Whatever you do, promise me you won't leave me alone."

Dino squeezed her hand. "You have nothing to worry about. We are in this together. I am not going to leave your side at all."

"Is that Greg and Doty down there?"

"Yes. Just watch where you are walking. Looks like there's a lot of garbage on the street."

"Good thing we are paper free." Madison took a piece of paper floating on the top of the water, which turned out to be one of their other neighbor's bank statements. "This is bad. The surge of water must have ripped open garbage bags."

"Forget about garbage bags. Look at the house across the street. The roof was ripped right off the top."

"Hey Dino," Greg called out before shaking Dino's hand. "Looks like you didn't evacuate either."

"No. We had fallen asleep. Besides, we didn't take the warning seriously. We shouldn't have stayed. Are you guys all right?"

"Barely," Doty said. "Greg refused to leave. We left before the last storm and not only did nothing happen, but our house got broken into. After we heard yelling last night, that's when we walked out onto the front porch and saw the water quickly building up. By then, it had been too late. The water already covered the car doors."

"What did you two do?" Greg asked.

"The whirling wind woke us up. When I got out of bed the water had already come up the stairs. Dino and I spent the night up in the crawl space."

"We have the full attic. So we ran up the stairs to watch from the tiny windows. You can't imagine the fear in me when I saw the waves coming. All I could do was scream. I felt the house shake as the waves hit, but by the grace of God we were spared. I guess this wasn't our time," Doty said.

"I totally agree with you." Turning around, Madison looked up and down the deserted street.

"Is there anyone else around?"

"Nope," Greg said. "Everyone evacuated. Looks like we were the only two that stayed around for the festivities."

"We are going to walk around to see what's going on. Do you want to come with us?" Dino asked.

"Sorry, Doty will never make it. Her arthritis has now settled in her legs."

Madison looked at the elderly couple. There wasn't much they could do for them. "We will send back help if we can find anyone. I wish we could do more."

"Just you two stopping by means the world to us. I'm sorry we never really got to know you kids," Doty said.

"Once everything gets back to normal, I'd like to have you over for dinner."

"We'd like that," Madison said.

Dino took hold of Madison's hand. "Are you ready? I'd like to get our friends help and see what is going on outside these streets."

"I'm ready. We'll see you later," Madison said, waving as they walked away. "I feel sorry for them. I hope they're going to be okay."

"I'm sure they will be. As soon as we see anyone, we'll send them back to help them."

They stopped when they hit a fork in the road.

"Which way do you want to go?" Dino asked.

"I know you're going to think this is crazy, it's a long walk, but what do you say we head to Shari's."

"Are you up to it? We had a pretty tough night."

"We have no other choice, Dino. We need to get to dry land."

"How do you know she's on dry land?"

"Because her house isn't in the evacuation zone."

"Let's go."

In some places they walked the water was up to their waists. When they turned to go up the hill, the water dropped down to their ankles. They passed a row of stores, one of them being a deli that had its front door open. Madison couldn't help but look inside. Food littered the room and the refrigerators laid face down on the floor. A few stores had their doors still shut with water lines three quarters of the way up their glass door and windows.

"This is a disaster," Madison whispered. "What if we can't get to Shari's house?"

"Sh." He covered her lips. "You of all people can't think negative thoughts. You always tell me to be positive. Well that applies to you too. We need to keep positive thoughts in our mind. We will make it to Shari's. I'll make certain of that."

"I hope you are right."

* * * *

"...and so the little giraffe found his way home to his mommy." Shari shut the book.

"Can you read me another story?" Thomas asked.

"In a little while."

"I'll read him a story," Sophia said.

Survival
219

"How about we go in the living room? I'll help you put the Ferris wheel together," Heather said, "if it's all right with you, Aunt Shari. I know it's big."

"Go ahead. I have a feeling today is going to be a long day."

"I'll make sure everything is cleaned up when we're done." Heather took Thomas off the bed. "Are you ready?"

"Am I ever. I love the Ferris wheel," Thomas sang running out of the room.

"Heather is so good with Thomas. She's a natural," Sophia said.

"I'm so lucky she made her way here. With my leg broken, I wouldn't have been able to do anything. She has always been an asset."

"Can I get you another bottle of water?"

"No. Maybe a diet soda. I feel like something sweet."

"Do you have any chocolate?"

"Wish I did. Maybe—" Shari stopped when the doorbell rang. "I bet Tommy forgot to take his key. Would you mind running downstairs to let him in?"

"Not at all."

Shari sighed in relief to be alone, if only for a few minutes. During the course of the past fifteen hours, everything seemed to have turned upside down, this being the first time since they were kids she hadn't spoken to Madison. But she could feel Madison's presence. She felt Madison was close.

She closed her eyes, but her attention was drawn to the conversation coming from downstairs. The voice had a slight familiarity, but she couldn't put her finger on it. What she did hear was the woman saying she had nowhere else to go. Her house had been wiped out by the storm.

"Bring the lady up. I'm sure she is standing out there in wet clothes," Shari called out.

"Really? You want to bring a stranger into your home?" Sophia asked.

"How could we turn anyone away during an emergency? You know my house has always been open to everyone."

Shari heard two sets of footsteps. The candles were still lit, however, she felt negativity surrounding her. Why did she feel like this?

Sophia stood in the doorway with a weird look on her face. When she stepped into the room, Shari's mouth dropped open. Now she knew where the negative energy came from. In her doorway stood Benita wearing black rubber boots. Her thick long curly hair was frizzed out, all over the place, and her clothes were wet, sticking to her body. Shari dropped her gaze to her hands, which shined with shiny purple nail polish.

"What the hell are you doing here, in my house?"

Benita stepped into the room. "I didn't have anywhere else to go. I'm here all alone. I have no family or friends to go to."

"You have got to be kidding me." Shari went to get off the bed, forgetting about her leg and screamed out in pain.

"Are you all right, Aunt Shari?" Heather asked, standing in the doorway.

"My leg. I forgot it was broken. That," she pointed at Benita, "is the bitch who burned down your store."

"Why did you burn down my mom's store?" Heather demanded. "Why would you do that to me and my mom. The store is our life."

"I didn't burn down your store," Benita said walking toward Shari's bed.

Shari held up her hand. "Don't you dare come any closer to me."

"Let me explain."

"There's nothing to explain, Benita. You drove us all crazy with your demented games. How could you try to destroy all our relationships? What in God's name were you thinking?" Shari screamed.

"Because of you, my mother is somewhere out there trying to get home," Heather added.

"This is the lady who caused all the damage?" Sophia asked. "The one who caused all that drama because of Fay's ex?"

"I'm sorry—"

Sophia leaped at Benita sending both women to the ground. Heather let out a scream causing both women to stop. "You two," she pointed, "get the hell up."

Shari looked from Heather, to Sophia and then Benita. The last time she saw Heather this angry was when her mother told her she had married Angelo. She had to keep Heather calm. The rage in her eyes scared her.

The look on Sophia's face said the same thing. Shari had to get this situation under control before something happened that would be life changing.

"Heather, do me a favor, go with Thomas. Make sure he doesn't come in here. I'll handle things from here."

"How are you going to handle things when your leg is broken?"

"I'm going to talk this out with the ladies. I will have no violence in my home." Shari opened her arms. "My home only gives off good karma. Since I can't get upstairs to my sacred room, this will be my space. Sophia, I'd like for you to go upstairs. Bring me down my purple and gold velvet table cloth."

"I can't leave you with her." She pointed to Benita.

"Don't worry. I will be okay. I will speak to her in my own way. So please, when you leave, shut my door. I will call you when we are done in here."

"I don't think—"

"Don't think. I'll be fine."

Shari waited for Sophia to close the door behind her before speaking. "I want you to pull up the chair over there, bring it over here to the side of the bed."

Benita's hazel eyes stayed fixed on Shari's. Pain, fright and nervousness leaked from her soul. Shari closed her eyes.

How do I make this lady understand I am alone? I lost everything. I have not one friend in this country. When I got out of jail I distanced myself from everyone. I made mistakes. I wanted to start a new life. But thoughts of the day I had the abortion keeps giving me nightmares. Angelo swore to me he loved me, would never leave me. When I told him I was pregnant, he flipped out, demanding I get an abortion, bringing me to a dirty back of a garage doctor. The doctor butchered me, leaving me unable to ever have a baby.

What can I do, say to let this woman know how sorry I am. I never meant to hurt any of them. I just flipped out when I saw he left me for Fay. If she throws me out, I don't know what I'm going to do. I'll have to return back home to my mom in Dominica, something I really don't want to do.

"Relax," Shari said. "I'm not going to throw you out of my house into the street. I don't operate that way. But what I want is answers."

Benita sat straight in the chair. Her right leg started shaking. Shari watched her place her hand on her knee to stop the nervous tick, but it continued.

"Please, the whole room is shaking. I am not going to do anything to you. As you can see," she pointed to her leg, "I have a broken leg. And I'm also not going to cast a spell on you. That isn't my style either. But I must warn you I have a lot of questions that need to be answered. The first being, why us? Why Fay? She didn't do anything to you."

Benita cleared her throat. "Angelo left me for her," she said in a deep Spanish accent. "He told me he loved me. Wanted to spend the rest of his life with me."

"Knowing Angelo's track record, I believe you. But what I don't understand is what changed to make him leave you to go to Fay."

"When I first met Angelo, I had just arrived here from the Dominican Republic. I ran into him at the airport when he was making a delivery. He helped me with my luggage to the cab station, then offered me a ride in his truck to save me money."

"I bet you regret accepting his invitation."

"Without a doubt." Benita took a deep breath, biting her bottom lip. However, the tears still escaped. "On the ride home, he asked me where I came from. I told him."

"He seemed intrigued. He wanted to know all about my hometown. So I described my friend's house. I didn't want to tell him I lived in a two bedroom shack with my mother, father, sister, along with my brother's wife and his four kids."

Benita's tears ran down her cheeks, with her nose dripping too. Shari took the little tissue pack from behind her pillow and handed it to her. She felt sorry for her. Angelo had a strange way of hurting people. Now she had this woman here feeling her pain.

"How did he find out you didn't live in a big house?"

"I showed him pictures when he insisted we go to Dominica on vacation. I didn't want to lie to him. I thought it best to come clean, tell him the truth."

"I can imagine his reaction."

Benita blew her nose, seeming to hesitate before continuing.

"He called me a lying whore before he left." Her voice cracked as tears poured from her eyes again. Shaking her head, she managed to regain her composure. "Two weeks later, I found myself pregnant. I went to the doctor. I was about two months along. When I told him he went ballistic, shoved me, slapped me across the face. The following day he took me for an abortion."

"Hey, I'm sorry."

"I had a botched up abortion. I'm sure you know the rest."

"I understand your frustrations, but I can't understand why you'd purposely try to destroy all our relationships."

"I don't have any answers. I don't know why I did what I did. Something snapped. Please, I'm so sorry. I never meant to hurt any of you. I was so happy when Angelo got put away for twenty-five years to life."

"We all were."

"My year in jail put a new perspective on my life. I took some courses, got my GED, and took medical billing classes. I started my job a month ago."

"That's great. But what I can't understand is why you burned down Fay's shop?"

Benita stared right into Shari's eyes and shrugged her shoulders. "I don't know why. I can't give you an answer."

"I'm not a fool. Tell me. What set you off? I need to know."

"Okay," Benita whispered. She dropped her head down, wiping the tears from her eyes before she spoke. "I drove to the shop with no intentions of burning it down. But once I got there, something happened. I felt rage, anger. Something snapped. I'm sorry. There is no explanation or reason for what I did."

"If Heather didn't run a half-hour late, you would have wound up killing her."

Benita pushed her hair off her face. "I didn't mean to."

"Not meaning to, wound up burning down a family business that had been passed down from one generation to another," Shari lashed out. "Do you realize how many people you have affected with your lack of judgment?"

"I didn't—"

"You threw a rock through the glass window. You sent all Fay's friends puzzle pieces. What did Madison, Cassie and I have to do with you?"

"Nothing."

"Be prepared not to be welcomed with open arms by any of my friends. I don't hate you because I don't know you. But I can assure you of one thing, I don't trust you."

"Okay."

"I would never put anyone out on the street, especially when they have nowhere to go. From what I'm hearing, out there is an absolute disaster. I will set you up with dry clothes. What you need to know is you will have to explain to each one of my friends why you were out to hurt them."

Shari lifted her tarot cards off the bed. "They will decide your future, if we call the police or not. Right now I'm ready to have your ass hauled in, but I know the police are out there in rescue mode."

"Thank you."

"Don't thank me yet. You will pay for what you did."

Shari and Benita looked at each other when they heard sirens in the distance getting closer to them. When the sirens stopped, she heard the front door open.

"Shari, help is here," Tommy yelled.

"The police are here?" Benita cried, turning toward the door.

Within seconds, her door opened. Tommy walked into her room along with two paramedics, who opened up a stretcher.

"The bridge opened. They will bring you to the hospital to set your leg."

"Are you coming with me? Heather and Sophia will watch Thomas."

"Yes. While the paramedics put you on the stretcher, I will talk to Thomas and let him know we will be right back."

"Thank you, Tommy."

The two men lifted her. She let out a scream. Once again, the pain radiated throughout her body, making going through labor seem like a breeze. One of the men gave her a shot. Within minutes, she felt lightheaded. *Oh yes. Now I'm feeling good.*

* * * *

After close to forty-eight hours of traveling and layovers, Fay's plane finally landed in Newark airport. But things weren't going to be easy. The plane sat on the tarmac for another hour, something to do with the terminal only running on a backup generator. Everyone on the plane had started going ballistic. The crew was out of beverages and the bathrooms were out of order.

"We are sorry for the inconvenience," said the male voice over the loudspeaker. "The good news is we are going to be pulling into the terminal in a few minutes. Thank you for your patience."

Everyone started clapping and cheering. This trip had been a long one for everyone, especially the layover in England. When the doors opened, Fay waited a couple of minutes for the plane to empty out. No sense in rushing. They would all be waiting for the luggage anyway.

Once she stepped off the plane, she did the sign of the cross. Reaching into her handbag, she took out her cell phone and dialed Heather. The phone rang twice before going to voice mail. Instead of leaving a message, she called again. Sometimes Heather needed a few minutes to locate her phone. Just like her, Heather had a bad habit of leaving her phone all over the place, then forgetting where she put it. Again, she found herself listening to voice mail. This time she left her message letting her know her plane had landed. She would be home soon.

While she waited for her luggage, two men spoke loud enough for her to overhear their conversation. Usually she wouldn't eavesdrop, but when they mentioned the shoreline of Staten Island being flooded out with casualties, she couldn't help but walk over to them.

"What's going on in Staten Island?" Fay asked the elder of the two men.

"Water. Plenty of it. I'm lucky my daughter was able to get in touch with me," the man said. "Most of the cell phone lines are down. My daughter lucked out. Her side of the street had their lights and telephone wires still up. She contacted me from her landline."

Fay covered her head with her hands. "What's going on? I heard a hurricane hit sometime last night."

"Hit is an understatement," the other man said. "The Jersey shore has been wiped out. From what my daughter is telling me, a lot of people who live by the shoreline are getting around Staten Island by boat. The ocean overflowed into the main streets."

"I'm on my way out there too. Hopefully there isn't a long line at the taxi stand."

"Forget about the taxi stand. We're on our way out to Staten Island. My daughter lives in Dongan Hills."

"I'm not too far from there. I'm going to my friend's house in Grasmere."

"Not a problem. We will take you where you need to go." He extended his hand. "I'm Gary," the elder of the two said, "this is my friend Brian."

"Nice to meet the two of you," Fay said, shaking both their hands. "I need to grab my luggage."

"So do we. We'll meet by gate K near the long-term parking lot." Gary looked at his watch. "I would have to guess it shouldn't take you any longer than an hour to get your luggage. But one of us will be there waiting for you."

"Thank you."

Fay walked to the luggage carousel. To make things easier for her, she had tied a lime green fishnet scarf around the handle. Crossing her arms, she patiently watched as bags went around on the carousel. The plane had been filled to capacity meaning there had to be over a hundred or so pieces that needed to be unloaded from the plane. Her luggage came flying out of the chute.

"Excuse me, excuse me." Fay made her way through the crowd of people standing in front of the carousel.

She pushed her way through when her first attempt at being polite didn't work. She grabbed her luggage and pushed her way through the crowd, walking with the rolling suitcase and her carry-on down to gate K.

At first when she got there, she didn't see either one of the men. Glancing at her watch, she would give them ten minutes before she ran across the airport to the taxi stand. She had to get home to Heather. Once she knew Heather was fine, she'd get in her car to check on her friends. Fifteen minutes later, she turned to walk toward the taxi ramp when the men came to meet her.

"Sorry. Got caught up getting our bags. Are you ready?"

"Yes, forty-eight hours ago."

Chapter Twelve

The fireman walked them up the stone walk. He opened the large wooden doors of the church for Cassie and Crystal. They stepped inside where two gray-haired elderly women greeted them.

"Welcome. I'm Betty, this is Doris. We will get you into dry clothes and help you settle in."

"Thank you," both women said together.

"You'll come with me," Betty said to Cassie.

"What about Crystal?"

"Doris will get her set up. We will meet in the church hall."

Cassie followed Betty into another room off the side of the chapel. Inside, partitions were put up with curtains closing off some of the rooms. Betty brought her over to a table where a variety of sweat pants, shirts, socks, sports bras, granny panties and black or white slip-on sneakers were lined up.

"The clothes are set up by size. Go grab what you need."

Cassie looked at the table, the big question being small or medium. She decided on the medium set of clothes. Comfort was the key at the moment. At the shoe section, she picked up a pair of black slip-on sneakers. Even as a kid, she hated the way brand new white sneakers looked.

"Are you done?" Betty asked.

"Ready to get out of these wet clothes, yes."

"Okay," she nodded her head, "follow me."

Cassie followed Betty through the maze of booths. Finally, she stopped in front of a cubicle where the curtain was drawn open. Linens along with a toothbrush and toothpaste box sat on a cot inside.

"This will be your space." Betty popped her head out of the booth. "You're booth is number fifty-seven. This is where you will keep your things and sleep at night."

"Thank you."

"I'll give you a few minutes to get ready. Come out when you're dressed."

"Thanks," Cassie said again.

Cassie shut the curtain. Her clothes were plastered onto her body. Taking off her jeans turned into a challenge, but brought back happy childhood memories with Sophia. One night in particular they had snuck out of Cassie's parent's summerhouse. They had taken off their stilettos to quietly walk down the wooden stairs. They went a few blocks away to meet the boys they had met earlier in the afternoon at the beach. But what they didn't expect was a huge thunderstorm. They ran home in their tight jeans, barefooted, to be greeted by both their mothers. Boy, did they get such an ass whipping when they got home. But to this day, she could remember trying to peel off her skintight jeans. Finally, she stepped out of her pants, leaving them inside out on the floor.

"Are you dressed?" Betty asked from the other side of the curtain.

"Almost."

"Here." Betty's hand came into the booth with a plastic bag and black marker pen. "Put your wet clothes into this bag. Don't forget to put your name on the bag. We will have your clothes ready for you later on."

"Thanks."

Cassie wrote her name on the bag, but knew she wouldn't be staying that long. Her intentions were to have a hot cup of coffee before leaving. She had to get back home. The closest place to check in with the girls would be Shari's. She could stop there before continuing on her journey back to her house.

Sliding open the curtain, she stepped out. Betty stood there smiling waiting for her.

"I bet you feel much better."

"Yes, I do." Cassie held out the bag. "Do I give this to you, or do I leave it on the cot?"

"I'll take it. If you follow me, I'll bring you into the church hall to meet up with your friend."

Cassie followed her through the maze. Once inside the hall, Betty disappeared. *Nice.* Walking around, she searched for Crystal. When she couldn't find her, she headed over to the table set up with coffee and food. That's where she found Crystal, sitting on the floor against the wall with a cup of coffee in her hand.

"Hey, can I join you?" Cassie asked, sitting next to her.

"Sure," Crystal replied, her eyes full of tears. "I still can't believe Harris is gone. We were making plans."

"I'm so sorry." Cassie put her arms around her.

"I'm all alone now. No one knew me and Harris had been together for over five years. We had to keep our relationship hidden or else I would have been reassigned to another precinct. Just forty-eight hours ago we were talking about setting a date. Instead, I will be sitting with his family at his wake and funeral. What am I going to do?" Crystal asked covering her face with her hands. "Harris has been my whole life."

"How did you meet him?" Cassie asked hoping to bring good memories afloat.

Crystal looked up, a slight smile appearing on her lips. "Harris saved my life."

"Tell me, please. I would love a happy thought."

"I had just left work. Instead of going straight home I decided to make a stop at a grocery store. On the way down Father Capodanno Boulevard, a car coming from the opposite direction jumped over the center island, slamming into me head-on."

"Oh my God."

"I tried to get out of the car, but my seat belt jammed with my leg crushed against the door. Somehow, I reached my cell phone on the seat to call for help."

"And Harris showed up."

"Yes. He cut my seat belt off, then got my leg free. When the ambulance arrived, the paramedics carried me to the stretcher."

"Wow. Not the most romantic first encounter."

"No. But to my surprise, he came to the hospital to visit me. He said he couldn't get me out of his mind. From the moment he lifted me out of the car, he knew I was his destiny."

Tears flowed from Cassie's eyes. Harris could have been anyone of them.

"Hey, why are you crying?" Crystal asked. "I'm the one who lost my boyfriend."

"That could have been any one of us. We were all standing in that storage room."

"Remember, happy thoughts." Crystal leaned forward to wipe Cassie's tears with the sleeve of her sweat shirt. "Tell me how you landed Antonio."

"While serving him with an order of protection."

"Now that's a romantic story to tell your grandchildren." Crystal giggled, but quickly her eyes watered with tears. "What am I going to do?"

"We're going to get the hell out of here. I have to make sure my cousin and friends are okay. Maybe we can use the phone here." Cassie stood, reaching her hand out to help Crystal up.

"Let's look for those ladies who helped us." Cassie looked around, but there were so many people walking around making it literally impossible to find anyone.

"Hey, there's a minister over there." She pointed to a man dressed in a black outfit. "Maybe he could help us."

In a flash, Cassie ran across the room with Crystal following behind, calling, "Excuse me, excuse me."

"How can I help you?" asked the tall, lean minister, touching her shoulder.

"Do you have a phone I can use to call to make sure my cousin is okay?"

"I'm sorry, but all the phones are down on this end of the island. From what I understand some parts of the island still have electricity, but seventy-five percent is in the dark."

"Oh dear." Crystal covered her mouth. "This isn't good."

"No it isn't." The minister folded his hands as if in prayer. "We have to be grateful to be here safe. If you would excuse me, we have more guests."

Cassie grabbed Crystal by the hand and led her across the room. "I have to get out of here. I can't sit here not knowing if my friends are safe."

"Oh, I don't think that's a good idea."

"I can't stay here. My friend Shari, lives about two miles away from here. I'm sure it's going to be a long walk, but I'm willing to give it a shot. Sitting around here worrying isn't going to help."

"If you're going, I'm coming along with you. I have no one. I'm scared. I don't want to stay here alone."

Cassie studied Crystal. The poor woman's eyes were barely open. "You look so tired. Are you sure you can make the trip on foot?"

"When was the last time you looked at yourself in the mirror?" Crystal snapped. "You look as though you are going to fall flat on your face too."

Cassie went to speak, lash out at her. Tell Crystal she doesn't have a clue to what she was talking about, but didn't. Crystal was absolutely right. The past twenty-four hours she hadn't gotten anymore than a few hours sleep, being in Antonio's arms, half scared to death. What she wouldn't give for a good night's sleep in her queen-sized bed, with those fine Egyptian sheets, that's if her house didn't get washed away.

"You're right. I'm in terrible shape too. But this is something I have to do. My cousin and friends are my whole life. They're the ones who are always there for me. Now I have to find them, make sure they are safe."

"We need to be there for one another." Crystal hugged Cassie. "I'm going to grab two bottles of water."

"I'll get us coffee to go."

"Perfect. On our walk, I'd love to hear about your friends. I'm literally here on my own. All my friends moved away when they got married to start their families."

"How about your parents?"

"Gone years ago. I've lived on my own in the Sun Garden Apartments off Bay Street in Rosebank."

Cassie froze in place. "Are you kidding me?"

"No, why?"

"I can't believe I never ran into you. My friend Shari has…"

"I know Shari. She does my hair."

"Damn. What a small world. I've been friends with Shari for years. I'm surprised we never crossed paths at the salon."

"I only go when my highlights fade," Crystal said, handing her a bottle of water. "Most times, I just trim the split ends off myself. I just don't have time to go every couple of weeks."

"Let's get out of here. We have a long journey." Cassie poured two cups of coffee. "Here you go."

Cassie walked over to the large wooden door. The moment she pushed the doors open to leave, the minister put his hand on the doors keeping them closed.

"I'm sorry, but I can't let you leave. The outside isn't what you remember it to be."

Cassie glanced over to Crystal who shrugged her shoulders.

"I appreciate everything you've done for us, Father, but I have to go home to check on my friends," Cassie said.

"Child," he touched Cassie's hand, "the streets are flooded. From what I understand, in some places the water level is still up to your waist. I think it would be in your best interest if you stayed here overnight."

"Sorry Father, but I have to get to my friends. They are my family. Once things get back to normal, I will be back with a donation to your parish. I wish I had something to give you now, but my handbag is floating somewhere down on Richmond Terrace."

"I wish you would rethink your decision."

"Sorry. But this is something I have to do." Cassie pushed open the wooden doors. "Thank you."

"Please don't go."

"What should we do?" Crystal asked.

"Say thank you, wave goodbye. We need to leave now if we are going to make it to Shari's before dark."

They both waved goodbye as they walked down the stone path back to the sidewalk. Cassie turned to look at the church before they began their journey. She hoped she wasn't making a mistake taking on this long walk without knowing what lies in their path. If anything happened to Crystal, she would never be able to forgive herself. Pivoting in her sneakers, she turned to go back in, but her feet wouldn't move. She had to make this journey.

"Are you ready?" she asked Crystal.

"I'm afraid, but yes."

"That's what I like to hear. I just hope we don't hit too many obstacles along the way."

They walked in the opposite direction of Richmond Terrace. Hopefully the water hadn't reached that high.

Cassie pointed toward her right. "How about we try walking down Van Duzer?"

"Let's give it a shot. The street is on a slight hill."

The women walked only four blocks before hitting water. Standing at the shallow end, they looked down the road where the cars were completely submerged. Cassie stopped, finished her coffee and placed the Styrofoam cup in the garbage pail before removing her shoes.

Crystal opened her arms. "What are you doing?"

"I'm going to walk through the water for as far as I can go, then I'll swim the rest of the way."

"Are you kidding me?"

"Not at all."

"Wait." Crystal grabbed Cassie's arm. "I have had some training by the police force in the event of an emergency, this being part of the training. We need to assess everything because once we go forward there is no turning back."

Cassie placed her hands on her hips. "Okay. Do your thing." She dropped her hands, taking a step back. "Tell me what I should do."

"I want you to take a moment to let your adrenaline come down."

"Why?"

"Take a deep breath. Tell me what you smell."

Cassie closed her eyes. Crystal was right. Her heart raced along with her mind in all different directions. She took a deep breath. *Damn, a foul odor lingered in the air*. Her eyes flew open.

"Do you smell that?"

"Yes. Also look at the water."

Cassie walked toward the start of the puddle. "Oh my God is that sewerage? The air smells like shit over here."

"Yes that's exactly what's floating in the water."

"We have to go a different way then. How about this way?" Cassie pointed in the opposite direction. "Maybe we can go up the hill off of St. Paul's Avenue and loop around to Targee."

"Let's give it a shot. You're right, we have to get out of here. I'm sure there are people who could use our help."

Cassie held up her sneakers. "Yeah, my friends." She pointed. "Look. There are people walking around over there, looks like a few blocks away. Maybe once we get through this water we will find a dry path out of here so we can get to Shari's."

Crystal took off her white sneakers before walking right into the shallow puddle. "Let go for it."

The water stayed pretty steady at around their ankles. At some points it rose up to their knees, before dropping back down to their ankles. At the halfway point, the water started getting deeper, leveling out around their waists.

Cassie looked at Crystal before taking off. "If the water gets too deep, I will try my best to swim the rest of the way. Are you all right with that?"

"I'm not the best swimmer, but as long as I know my feet will eventually touch the street, I have no problem giving it a shot."

"Let's go for it."

The first three blocks they walked, the water had only reached a little higher than their ankles, but as they approached the park, the water got deeper, in some places up to their waists. Cassie concentrated on where she stepped. There was broken glass on the floor and small appliances, which possibly washed out of someone's house along with sewerage. At some points the smell became so unbearable, Cassie vomited.

Maybe she had made the wrong decision leaving. They did have a warm bed at the church, but her friends meant the world to her. She wouldn't be able to rest until she knew everyone was okay.

"Damn it, I dropped a sneaker," Crystal's voice shrilled.

"Where?"

"Somewhere around here."

"Don't worry, I'll find it. The sneaker has to be somewhere in the immediate area."

"I hope so, but I can feel the current pulling toward Bay Street."

"Let's backtrack for a bit. If we can't find it, I'll give you my sneakers."

Crystal had been right. She could feel the undertow pulling them, giving them a hard time.

"Forget about the sneaker. We have to keep going or else we are never going to make it out of this," Cassie said. "I can feel the water whirlpooling around my feet."

"I'm scared, Cassie. I don't think I can continue."

"Hello." Cassie extended her arms into a circle. "We are in the middle of water. What do you want to do? Now pull yourself together. This is the only way out of here. Besides, you told me you were trained for things like this, so let's get going now."

Crystal took her other sneaker and threw it into the water. "Okay, forget about the sneakers."

Cassie bit her tongue. The last thing she wanted to do is start arguing. The fear running through her body had raised her adrenaline. She would make it through the water to the other side. The level seemed to be going down as they walked, the current slowing up.

Looking over her shoulder, she saw tears in Crystal's eyes. That's why she had to remain strong, not show her fear.

"Are you all right?" Cassie asked, when Crystal stopped walking.

"Yes. I am just saying a prayer."

"Okay."

Crystal positioned her hand straight ahead. "Looks like we only have to walk another few blocks. I can see the street."

"Yes, you're right." Cassie started walking with Crystal beside her. "Look where the waterline is now on us," she said, pointing to her upper thighs. "It's going down. I just wish there would have been an easier way."

"We're almost there. But a funny thing, I feel as if Harris is right here with me."

"I believe you. I know my mom is here with me."

"I know you said happy thoughts. But I'd feel so much better reciting my wedding vows, I had written."

"You remember them?"

Crystal smiled. "Yeah. I've been practicing them for weeks."

"Okay, I'd love to hear them."

Crystal looked up to the sky and blew a kiss. "Because of you time stands still when we embrace. A stormy day takes on new meaning. The sound of rain pounding on the pavement, day darkened by the gray sky, but light shines right through you. I can see your eyes through the bright flame of burning candles. Because of you I am able to cope with my fears, turning to you in darkness, knowing the dark clouds will rise and sunshine will break through. Because of you my heart will remain forever young. Being with you, our passion will always feel like the first time. Because of you I no longer cry. Your presence is always with me mind, body and soul. Because of you I learned to love, accepted being loved, by giving you all the love inside of me."

As Crystal recited her vows, Cassie kept her eyes on her. She hoped she didn't breakdown. But she was surprised to have gotten the opposite response. Saying the vows had given her the strength to continue their journey to safety.

"Beautiful. You would have brought tears to Harris's eyes."

"I know." Crystal looked around. "We made it. We got to the other side in one piece."

"Yes. Hopefully the rest of the journey to Shari's won't be as bad."

"Excuse me," a deep voice said.

Both women turned around.

"We are asking everyone to remain in their homes," said the tall lanky police officer.

"That's where we are heading. We were both rescued from the police precinct. I'm making my way home now. We had to walk through the water to get here."

"I need to see your ID."

Cassie opened her arms. "Sir, I don't have any ID nor do I have money."

"And you?" he asked Crystal.

"My boyfriend, Detective Harris Winters, just died in an effort to save us. Her boyfriend is Detective Antonio Palencia, who along with Detective Vic Mariano are down on Richmond Terrace helping in the rescue of people trapped in their homes. Do you have any other questions?"

"I have no time to stand here arguing with you ladies. Please get to your destination and stay there."

"We will, officer. Thank you."

On this side of the water, the street remained dry, most of the houses unmarred. The biggest damage had been the downed trees, many of them falling through people's roofs. The neighborhood looked like a ghost town. No one was out. The buzzing noise of generators could be heard along with the continuing sound of sirens.

"How much farther to Shari's?"

"I'd say around another mile as long as we don't hit anymore water. Are you okay?"

"Yes. We've come this far, I don't plan to stop now."

Chapter Thirteen

Fay followed Gary and Brian into the parking lot, with each man carrying a piece of her luggage along with theirs. All the jewelry and scarves she had packed in her suitcase along with the ones she had sent back were now meaningless. Her family legacy had been taken away from her.

"What the hell do you have in this suitcase?" Gary asked stopping for a few minutes. "I feel like I am pulling a bag of bricks."

"I brought home cotton and silk fabric from Italy."

"Why the hell didn't you mail the fabric back home?" Brian asked pushing his blond hair behind his ears.

"I did. This is the last thing I picked up before I left." Fay slid her carry-on bag off Brian's shoulder. "I have a full plate to deal with when I get home. The first thing is making sure my daughter is safe."

"All you had to do is call," Gary said walking again.

Fay frowned. "Not anymore. I called so many times I only have two percent of my battery left."

"Here you go." Brian reached into his jacket pocket, handing her his cell phone. "Go ahead, try."

Fay tapped Heather's number into the phone. To her surprise, this time the phone rang six times before going to voice mail. Next she dialed each of her friends. On the landlines, she received a busy signal, while the cell phones all rang before going to voice mail too. Fay took this as a good sign.

"Wow," Brian said. "Look at the water over there in the parking lot. Good thing we were in the long-term lot."

"You ain't kidding," Gary said.

Fay did the sign of the cross while looking up at the sky. "Thank the Lord." She glanced at her watch, tapping the face. "Hopefully, if there isn't any traffic, we can arrive there in a half-hour."

"Don't get your hopes up, kiddo. I don't like what I'm seeing already."

"Why do you say that?" Fay asked stopping at the navy blue BMW.

"Looks like there are floods all over the place." Gary opened the trunk and rearranged the luggage around the two cases of iced tea.

Fay bit her tongue. She would've opened the trunk and tossed the bags in. Watching Gary put the luggage into the trunk had been the least of her problems. In the car, she sat in the middle of the back seat as Brian drove down the turnpike at forty miles an hour. Cars passed them, shaking the car as they sped by. But the drive on the turnpike came to a complete halt another mile down the road. The six lane operation had turned into just one. The message board flashed informing drivers that multiple canals had overflowed blocking the highway, sending everyone into one lane.

"This is beat," Gary commented placing his hand over Brian's on the hand rest. "I think we should get off, stop for some food. Hopefully by then the traffic would've died down a little."

"Works for me," Brian said. "I have never seen this much traffic before."

"Guys, I need to get home."

"Yes, so do we. We both have families we are worried about. But there is nothing we can do."

Gary pointed straight ahead. "Look, the traffic goes on for miles. Besides, we are exhausted after the long trip. I'm sure you can go for a cup of coffee."

Fay rolled her eyes. "I'd rather sit in the traffic, but since you're driving I guess I'll have to go along for a cup of coffee."

"Good." Gary squeezed his way over to the right lane and took the ramp to the food court.

The lot didn't have one vacant spot. Gary drove around for over an hour before finding one. Fay stared at the highway, which stood at a complete halt. The traffic moved faster in the parking lot. Once inside the food court, Fay went right over to the coffee shop.

"What can I get you," the young girl asked.

"French vanilla hot latte, sugar, extra whipped cream." Fay pointed at the glass showcase. "I'll also have one of those multigrain bagels with low fat cream cheese."

"A girl after my own heart." Brian chuckled.

Fay smiled. After the girl handed her the bag, she brought it into the small little area off in the corner. The television caught her eye with pictures of Staten Island. Fay walked closer to the television and sat down, along with Gary and Brian.

Fay pointed. "Oh my God. There is South Beach. What happened to the beach, the boardwalk, the street? The street is now part of the ocean."

"This is unbelievable. I'm hoping the water didn't reach my house," Gary said.

"You live close to the shoreline?" Fay asked.

"No. We live above the boulevard," Gary said.

"The problem is there is a creek a few blocks away. In the past when the water rises, the creek overflows down to our block, into our basement."

"That's why Brian put in two sub-pumps."

"You get that much water?" Fay asked.

Gary and Brian looked at each other nodding their heads.

"When we moved in together, Gary had built rooms down in the basement for us to use as storage."

"If my house survived the storm, that would be a miracle. My block is prone to floods too." Fay put her head down when her eyes started watering. "To be honest, I don't know what I'm walking home to. My friends had called me two days ago telling me my family owned store, passed down from one generation to another, burned down. I don't know the extent of how bad, if I lost everything, or if there is anything left to salvage."

"Think positive," Brian said. "This is hard for all of us. I'm hoping we're not walking into a disaster either."

"I don't think I can handle much more of anything. These past few years have been horrendous for me." Fay held out her hand. "Please don't think I'm looking for sympathy, because I'm not."

"I wasn't planning on giving you any. We," Brian pointed to him and Gary, "have had our own drama. Imagine us telling our wives we are gay."

"Now admitting one's sexuality isn't out of the ordinary."

"How about we were brother-in-laws. We fell in love with each other when we went on vacation with our wives," Brian said, resting his hand on Gary's shoulder.

"While the ladies were sitting out at the pool all day, we were upstairs in the bedroom…"

"Sorry guys." Fay held up her hand. "Too much information for me. I don't have anything against anyone's sexual preference. I'm just old-fashioned. What happens in the bedroom stays in the bedroom."

"We can understand that," Brian said. "I'm sorry if we made you feel uncomfortable."

"No," she shook her head, "not at all. My main concern now is making sure my daughter is fine. I couldn't live with myself if something happened to her."

"I'm sure she's fine."

"Let's get out of here." Brian stood. "Let's get her home to her daughter."

"Look at the traffic. I think we should wait it out," Gary insisted.

"We both know our kids are okay. If we didn't, we'd be sitting in that traffic hoping it opened up so we can get home. Correct me if I'm wrong."

Gary didn't answer. He stood taking his coffee and bag of donuts with him.

"Thanks guys." Fay sipped her latte. "You can't believe how much this means to me. If I would have gotten to talk to my daughter, I would have been content in waiting for the traffic to let up."

"Not a problem. I promise to get you home as soon as I can," Brian said.

* * * *

When Dino came to a complete halt and sat down on a brick wall in front of someone's house, Madison's heart started palpitating. They were only three blocks away from Shari's, so Dino stopping meant something was wrong.

Madison took a deep breath. She had to find out what was bothering Dino, without letting on.

"Break time?" she asked sitting next to him.

"Yes. My feet are starting to hurt. We've been walking with wet sneakers for over an hour."

Sitting next to him, she heard his heavy breathing. Not a good sign. "You're right. We should've taken a break along the way."

"Nah, I'm okay."

"No you're not," she snapped.

Dino's eyes narrowed. "Are you telling me how I feel?"

"Honestly, yes. Even your words are mumbled."

"I'm out of breath. Walking though the water was a little too much for me," he admitted. Dino took a deep breath, slowly exhaling. "Baby, I'll be okay. Just give me a few minutes before we continue."

Madison turned sideways. "Promise me you won't leave me. I don't think I could survive without you."

"I'm doing my best to keep my health intact. I'm doing everything the doctor told me. Come on babe," he took her hand in his, "I haven't had a beer in weeks, or any alcoholic beverages for that matter."

"As soon as we get to Shari's, I promise I will personally pop open a bottle of beer for you."

"I'm going to hold you to that."

"Believe me, I need one too." Madison lifted his hand and placed it on her heart. "What are we going to do, Dino? Our house is destroyed."

"Shh, it's okay." Dino put his arms around her, rocking her. "You'll see. Everything is going to be okay. Our house only had possessions inside. All the memories are embedded in our hearts. Those are the things the storm couldn't take away from us."

"I know, but we lost your studio. Everything you worked hard for."

"The equipment, yes. But all the work, no. I have everything saved in cyber space, the music, the magazine. Everything else can be replaced. Besides, we've been talking about moving. Maybe now's the time to find our retirement home."

"Pennsylvania?"

Dino chuckled. "You're telling me you are going to leave your friends."

Madison stood, holding her hands out to Dino who joined her. "I would do anything or go anywhere to be with you."

"Then the decision is made. Once things calm down, we will look at all our options."

Dino put his arms around her shoulders, crushing her against him, kissing the top of her head. A car sped down the block through the puddles on Fingerboard Road, splashing water all over them, causing them to jump apart.

"Asshole," Madison screamed in the middle of the street.

"Hey, don't get nuts. We are already wet."

"I'm just on edge," she said, hands on hips.

"Hey," he waved his finger back and forth, "I don't like that stance. There isn't anything you can do about what's happened." Reaching for her hand, he took it in his.

"Everything will turn out perfect as long as we are together."

"Your business. Most of your clientele comes from New York."

"Doesn't matter." He reached out, covering her lips with his finger. "Let's take things one day at a time. The most important thing is we are here together. The rest will fall into place."

Madison stepped back. "You're right. We have the magazine, we have each other. I'm just frazzled with everything going on. I'm so thankful for what we have."

"Amen." Dino took her hand in his. "All we have to do now is get through one more big puddle." He pointed ahead.

"I can't wait to get to Shari's so I can jump into the shower, then get into some dry clothes."

"I hope her house is okay."

"She wasn't in the evacuation zone. Besides, she doesn't have a basement either. And knowing Tommy, he covered the floor to ceiling windows just in case."

"I have to agree with you. Tommy is a good man. I'm sure Shari is safe at home with Thomas."

"You're right. He would make sure nothing happened to his family."

Madison walked down the block in ankle deep water with Dino. That part of the block always got puddles especially during a heavy rainstorm, never ankle deep, but enough to get your shoes wet.

"I see Shari's house." Madison pointed, sighing. "I can't tell you how relieved I am."

"Me to," Dino said. "I'm starting to get really tired."

"Are you all right? Do you want to sit down on the curb for a couple of minutes?" she asked touching his shoulder.

"No. We're almost there. Once we get there I'll sit down for a few."

Madison wanted to run down the street to Shari's house, but resisted the temptation of warm shelter and dry clothes for her husband. During this whole disaster the only thing she'd worried about was keeping Dino calm. Their ordeal with his open-heart surgery last year had been enough of a scare for one lifetime.

Madison took a deep breath standing outside the shop. They had been right. Tommy had all the windows boarded up. Looking around, she didn't see Tommy's jeep. She hoped he wasn't out looking for them. But then again, he would have never made it through the waist high water that barricaded the blocks surrounding their house.

"I got the bell," Dino said.

They waited a few minutes before ringing the bell again. This time the door opened with Heather greeting them.

"I am so glad you are all right, Aunt Madison." Heather hugged both of them. "There is so much going on you can't even imagine."

"Tell me about it." Madison closed and locked the front door before walking up the stairs behind Dino. When she reached the top, she looked around. Usually Shari would be waiting for her with some sort of alcoholic beverage in her hand for her. "Where's Shari?"

"Shari's fine," Heather said not looking her in the eyes.

"Something happened. Tell me."

"She ran down the stairs, tripped, and broke her leg."

"She what? Oh my God where is she?"

"She went with Tommy to the hospital," Sophia said walking into the kitchen. "She has either a broken left leg or ankle. Nothing too serious."

"Oh thank God." Madison hugged Sophia. "When did you get here?"

"A little while ago."

"We didn't see your car," Dino added.

"How I got here is another story."

"Did you walk from your apartment?" Madison asked.

"Ah, no. I walked from a shelter off Father Capodanno. I got stuck at the restaurant in the middle of the hurricane. A wave came through the banquet room. I spent some time sleeping in the chandelier."

"No way," Dino said.

"How did you get out of the light?"

"By the time I woke up, the water calmed down. I climbed down onto a table, that being just the beginning of my journey, part of which had me in shoulder deep water." Sophia zipped her sweat shirt. "*Brr.* I still can't get the chill out of my body. To top that, I got rescued by boat."

"By boat?"

"Yeah, can you imagine? The water's so deep on Father Capodanno Boulevard, you couldn't walk through it. If the fireman didn't come, I would still be hanging onto the railing outside on the deck. I have never been so scared my whole entire life. When my feet hit dry payment I wanted to kiss the ground."

"We were stuck in our crawl space. Our whole first floor, totally wiped out," said Madison.

"Geez, I'm really sorry to hear that. What about the second floor?" Sophia asked crossing her arms.

"Because we don't have a basement, the water came up the stairs to the bedrooms. I think at one point the water must have been higher than the bed," said Dino.

"I'm hoping I can save most of the things in the closet. The stuff in the crawl space wasn't affected at all," Madison explained.

"Thank God. Coffee?" Sophia asked while she poured coffee into two paper cups.

"Yes. With a shot of brandy in both of them." Dino opened the cabinet and took out the bottle. He turned to Madison. "I think we both deserve it."

Madison glared at Dino. The look on his face was so pathetic she didn't have the heart to tell him no. "I think you're right." She grinned. "The past twenty-four hours have been torturous. I think a drink would be exactly what the doctor ordered."

"I agree with her." Sophia handed them their cups.

Dino opened the bottle and poured a generous amount of brandy into their cups before handing Madison hers. "Sorry, sweetheart, but this ordeal needs extra alcohol."

"I agree." She sipped her coffee. "I'm going to take my coffee upstairs. I am in desperate need of a hot bath."

"Wait." Heather went to grab her arm, but Madison had already walked into the living room.

Her attention went directly to Thomas who sat in front of the television playing with his blocks singing nursery rhymes along with the show.

She walked over to kiss the top of his head. "Hi Thomas."

Thomas gave her a quick kiss on the cheek before returning his attention to the television. She couldn't help but smile. If only she were a few years younger. Who was she kidding, ten years ago she would have insisted they had a baby. But now age played a big part. Once she'd hit her mid-forties, she'd started going through her changes. She'd be content in spending the rest of her life with Dino.

"I'm heading to the bathroom." Sophia and Heather stared at her with a look of concern on their faces. "Hey, what's wrong?" she asked looking from one to the other.

"Would you mind if I had another cup of coffee?"

Madison turned around coming face to face with Benita. Her eyes bulged wide open and her jaw dropped. After a few moments of silence, Madison turned around to look at the others.

"What is she doing here? She tried to destroy us," Madison lashed out. "What do you want from us now?"

"I don't want anything. I came here because I have nowhere else to go. I explained everything to Shari. She's all right with me being here."

"Oh, no." Madison jerked her head back and forth. "I don't believe it. You tried to destroy my marriage."

"What are you talking about?" Dino asked, coming into the room.

"This bitch sent Shari, Cassie and I puzzle pieces using pictures of us in compromising positions."

Dino walked over to her. "Why didn't you tell me? What kind of pictures?"

"Old pictures of me and Sal that she made into puzzle pieces. Fay got the worst of it though—a rock through the store's window."

"And she's here?" Dino asked his voice raising a notch. "Does Shari know? Because I bet she would have thrown her right out on her ass."

"Shari knows," Heather said.

"I find this so hard to believe. You really have some nerve." Madison approached Benita. "How could you even show your face around here knowing what you did?"

"I'm sorry for what I've done," Benita said in a whisper. "I shouldn't have done that to you."

"But the store. How could you burn down the store? Oh my God, what is Shari thinking?"

"She forgave me."

"I'm sure she did because she believes in positive karma. But me," Madison pointed to herself, "I believe if you do something to hurt someone, you should pay for it in deuces."

"No, Aunt Madison. This isn't you talking. I've never seen you look this mad."

"I am. This woman tried to single-handedly ruin all our relationships."

"I would have never believed it," said Dino, putting his hands on her shoulders. "You can tell me anything. But I don't understand why?" Turning to Benita, he pointed his finger inches from her face. "Shame on you. To think after what you have done to these ladies, Shari still let you into her house."

As Dino took her in his arms, Madison kept her eyes on Benita who didn't utter a word. Benita being there totally upset her. They were lucky to be alive and now this.

She pulled out of Dino's arms to face Benita. "In all honesty, I can't deal with you. We still don't know if Cassie and Fay are okay. And until I see Shari for myself, I won't be able to rest."

"You won't have to wait any longer."

They all turned around. Shari stood in the doorway of the living room on crutches, her left leg in a cast.

"Are you all right?" Madison covered her mouth with her hand.

"I'll be fine after I hear the popping open of a bottle of beer."

"Hey, you know what the doctor said. No alcoholic drinks," Tommy said.

"I'll go get you a beer," Sophia said. "I'm going to get all of us a beer. This has been one hell of a day."

"Yes it has," Madison said emphasizing each word.

"I'll take my beer." Dino swiped the opened bottle out of Sophia's hand. "Come on, Tommy. I know the tone in Madison's voice. The atmosphere isn't going to get any better in here."

"I'll grab Thomas. We'll watch television in the other room."

"That's it on the beer," Madison lashed out at Dino. "Your first and last one. I don't need to be back at the hospital with you."

Madison took a long slug out of the bottle along with the others. Shari sat on the living room couch with her leg up on the table. Heather grabbed a pillow off the couch, placing it under her cast.

"Sit," Shari said tapping each side of her.

Sophia sat down with Madison following on the right side of Shari, Benita on the love seat across from them, Heather in Tommy's recliner.

"Before any of you start yelling, especially you," she tapped Madison's leg, "I want to explain to you why Benita is here with us."

Madison crossed her arms. "This is an explanation I am dying to hear. That woman tried to ruin our lives," she said as the volume of her voice raised three decibels.

"I know. But before we get into this, I need to know, how did you get here? I didn't see your car out there. We tried to pass your house but a deep puddle of water stopped us from proceeding."

"My car is in a neighbor's yard on its side, my house is ruined. We walked here. Last night we were stuck upstairs in the crawl space all night." Tears escaped from her eyes. "Everything is gone, ruined on the first floor. All the antique furniture, Dino's studio, completely wiped out. The water rose over my bed."

"Why didn't you evacuate? The mayor ordered evacuations all along the coastline. The news kept giving a list of all the areas in the mandatory evacuation areas."

"We weren't watching TV." Madison glanced over at Benita who sat expressionless. She wanted to leap off the couch and punch her in the face. *Bitch.* But instead she bit her tongue.

"What the hell? I told you earlier there was a huge storm coming in."

"I hate talking in front of her." She pointed at Benita.

"Benita isn't going anywhere right now nor is she my concern," Shari said.

"I agree," Sophia said, with Heather nodding her head in agreement.

"Sorry," Benita whispered.

"Start talking," Shari ordered.

"Dino's problem is no longer an issue," Madison said.

"What problem?" Sophia asked.

Madison looked from Sophia to Shari to Heather. *This has turned into such an awkward situation.*

"Oh okay. That's wonderful," Shari said tapping Madison's arm.

"I don't understand," Sophia said again.

This time Madison shoved her right hand between her legs. "Do you all get it now?" she asked feeling heat rise in her face.

"Oh," Sophia said. "Time for a refill along with a subject change."

"Agreed." Heather stood. "I'll get the beers."

Madison knew she volunteered because she didn't want to be in the middle of the argument that was about to take place. Now that she explained herself, she wanted answers on why Benita was sitting in the middle of Shari's living room when she knew Shari hated her just as much as the rest of them.

"Did anyone hear from Cassie or Fay?" Sophia asked.

"Nope. Neither one of them has their phone on either," answered Shari.

"They may have no power. We lost our power. My cell phone has no juice now. It went dead earlier this morning. But even at that, all I got was all circuits are busy when I tried to get a hold of you," Madison said.

"Mine must have washed out to sea," Sophia said. "After the waves hit, I found myself waking up on a chandelier and lucky enough not to be pulled out into the ocean."

"Wow," Madison said. "That's horrible."

"What's even worse is the man who came to warn me about the high waves, died. I saw his body floating in the water left from the storm."

Shari covered her cheeks with her hands. "Oh dear God."

"Oh Sophia, that's horrible." Heather handed her the first beer.

"You *are* lucky to be alive," Madison said.

Heather handed Madison her beer. "So are you. We are all lucky to be alive. My house is destroyed too. I walked here through waist high puddles at times."

"That's what I mean." Shari wiggled her toes in her cast. "We are all alive and well. Sure Benita is our foe, but until I know all my friends are alive and safe, I can't do or say anything negative that will cause bad karma. Once our circle of friends is all together, we will deal with the evil Benita has bestowed upon us.

Chapter Fourteen

The traffic continued to be horrendous. No matter which way Brian went, they still sat bumper to bumper. After what seemed like hours, when they couldn't cross the Goethal's Bridge, they finally made their way to the Outerbridge Crossing. The traffic was backed down Interstate 278 for miles.

Brian took the right lane as they crawled over the bridge. But the worst part was looking at the water underneath the bridge that extended onto the coastline. It surrounded houses long into the distance.

"Oh wow." Gary opened his window. "Look Fay. Are those men in rowboats?"

Fay squinted, straining to look. Finally, she saw the boats Gary was talking about. "I can't believe it. There are people in them."

"And this is only the canal between Jersey and Staten Island. I wonder what kind of damage there is at South Beach and Midland Beach," Gary said rolling up his window.

"I can just imagine," Brian said. "Thank God we don't live close to the shoreline."

"I live close to the shoreline." Fay leaned up, resting her hands on both Brian and Gary's seat.

"Where are you?" Brian asked.

"I'm behind the wetlands by the park and ride lot."

"You should be okay. I doubt the water reached that far up," Gary said.

"I hope not," said Brian, "We just got finished renovating our house. I finally made the den into a pool room."

"Yeah. Imagine I had to marry him to get my dream room."

Brian leaned over and kissed him. "Oh stop it. I always give you what you want."

Fay sat back down behind Gary blocking out their love spat. Her main concern was her daughter. Every time she called Heather's phone it went directly to voice mail, causing her to worry even more. Heather never shut off her cell phone, neither did Madison or Shari. Until she saw her friends in the flesh, she wouldn't be able to rest.

Considering everything that had happened, she wondered how soon Gavino would come to the States to visit. From the moment she met him in the village circle in Sicily, she fell in love with him, a feeling she never had with any man in her life.

Gavino had been her godsend. The morning she met him, she had been wandering around the fabric store in town holding four five-foot long cardboard cylinders draped with the finest silks and cottons. Gavino accidently bumped into her causing the cylinders to fall out of her hands, onto the cobblestone floor. He spoke to her in Italian, she answered in English. After helping her pick up the cylinders, he paid for the material. As they walked back into the town square he asked her out for lunch, she accepted.

For the first few weeks, they developed a friendship. Two months later, their friendship turned into a love affair. They were getting ready to leave for Paris for a few days when she got the phone call from Shari about her store.

With all her worrying about Heather, she totally forgot about the store. Everything her family had worked for had been destroyed. From the pictures Shari had sent her, everything had been destroyed. She hoped some of the jewelry she had stored could be saved.

The last few deliveries she had received before her vacation she had taken home with her because the scarves and shirts were so wrinkled she couldn't put them out. She never did have time to iron them or go through the whole big box of jewelry she had placed in the spare bedroom.

All the boxes she had sent from Naples went to Shari's shop. Hopefully the hurricane didn't destroy the salon. But Shari had said she put them up in her attic where they would be safe. She hoped the clothes didn't wind up smelling like incense. Guess she would find out in a bit.

Her phone beeped, despite only having two percent of battery left. She retrieved it from her handbag. Gavino had sent her a text.

I miss you already. Call me when you get home.

Fay smiled. Gavino promised to come spend a few months with her. She was also able to reinstate her Italian citizenship. Now she could travel back and forth to Italy without having to worry about extending her paperwork. Her parents never told her she had duel citizenship. She didn't even know they were still citizens.

Brian jammed on the breaks, causing Fay to bang her head against the back of Gary's seat.

"Sorry guys," Brian said. "Look at the water. Damn, it's almost as high as the car doors a block down."

"What the hell happened here? Looks like a battle zone," Fay cried. "How the hell are we going to get to the other side of the island?"

"Don't worry, I will get you home," Brian said.

"It's killing me not knowing if my daughter is okay. I just need to hear her voice."

"I promise you I will have you home as soon as I can. I just have to drive slow and easy. Looks like the power is out."

Gary pointed down the side street. "Look at the water. How the hell did it get this far up from the bay?"

Shocked, Fay couldn't answer. Hylan Boulevard had a layer of sand covering the six lane road. Could it be the water came all the way from the shoreline?

"I can't believe the lights and some traffic lights are out." Fay fiddled with her phone. "I have no service again."

She wasn't going to make herself crazy. She'd be home within a half-hour.

It took close to an hour before they even made it halfway across the island. Hylan Boulevard had been turned into a disaster area. By the time they got to Guyon Avenue, the devastation to the houses below the boulevard was disturbingly evident. The traffic light was out at Hylan

Boulevard–Guyon Avenue, a major intersection. All Fay saw was dirty water and sand. They drove a little farther down the boulevard until they couldn't anymore. The police had blocked off Hylan Boulevard after Lincoln Avenue, for that part of the boulevard had been flooded out too.

When they reached the intersection where the police stood behind blue barriers in the middle of the street directing traffic, Gary rolled down his window. "How far down does the water go?"

"Looks as if it goes down past Seaview Avenue," the police officer responded.

"Oh. That's not good."

"This storm hit Staten Island hard. The diner got flooded out. The takeout place across the street from it is destroyed. The tables floated three blocks up the road," said the officer.

"Oh my God." Fay held her face between her hands. "That's terrible."

"Terrible isn't the word. We live very close to the diner," Brian said.

"Below the boulevard is wiped out. Eighty-five percent of the houses by the water were destroyed. Some were ripped off their foundation." The officer shook his head.

Tears rolled down Fay's cheeks. "I have to get home. I need to know my daughter is okay. Can we get through toward the Verrazano Bridge?"

"You will have to do some weeding up and down streets. Just be cautious. There are blackouts throughout the island."

"Thank you, officer." Gary rolled up his window. "We have an assignment, Brian."

"And what is that?"

"We have to get Fay home no matter how long it takes us."

They drove around for the next hour. They would get so far and then reach water causing them to detour a mile out of the way. Fay sat in the back seat quietly as anxiety ate at her nerves. Words couldn't describe what she saw. The corner of Midland Avenue and Hylan Boulevard had turned into a lake. The water reached up to the street sign.

"I don't think I'm going to be able to get you to your house," Brian said. "Can we drop you anywhere else?"

"I would think the only one of my friends who shouldn't have been affected is Shari, who lives above her beauty parlor on Fingerboard Road."

"That might be doable. I'll try to get myself up to Richmond Road."

"Thank you. I appreciate you going out of the way for me. I am a wreck not knowing if my daughter is okay," Fay repeated again, with tears in her eyes.

"Don't start that crying shit again," Gary warned her. "We will get you home, but I can't take the whining and crying."

"Give her a break," Brian said. "At least you spoke to your kids."

Fay sat back in her seat. After a few diversions up and down streets, Brian finally reached Richmond Road. From there, even though they drove at a crawl, they made it out to the service road where the traffic stood at a standstill on both the highway and service road.

An hour later, they reached Fingerboard Road. The streets of Fort Wadsworth were water free. They rode down Fingerboard Road getting stuck at the light. Once they crossed Tompkins Avenue, Fay's heart started pounding.

"Her house is right there." She pointed to the left.

Brian stopped the car in the middle of the street. He popped the trunk and took out her suitcases. "Do you have anything else?"

"Nope, just my handbag." Fay opened the car door. "Thank you, Gary."

Gary opened the car door. "You're welcome." He reached his hand out to shake hers, but instead Fay hugged him.

"I can't thank you enough. I hope we see each other again under better circumstances."

"You can count on it," Gary said.

Fay stepped back, turning around to face Brian who stood with her two bags.

"I want to make sure your friend is home before I leave."

"Thank you."

Fay ran across the street with Brian following behind. The outside windows were all boarded up. She skipped to the front door and banged multiple times on the doorbell until she heard someone yell, "I'm coming."

The front door opened. "Fay's here," Tommy yelled up the stairs.

Before she could speak, she saw Heather coming at her with tears in her eyes. She threw her arms around her neck as they both wept.

Fay took a step back. "Thank God, you are okay."

"I was just about to say the same thing to you."

"Hey, I have to get going," Brian said. "I can see Gary getting all bent out of shape from here."

"I'll take her bags." Tommy reached into his pocket and handed him a twenty. "Thank you."

Brian pushed Tommy's hand away. "Hey, man. I'm not car service. We met her at the airport in despair. We were all going to Staten Island, so we took her along with us."

Tommy shook his hand. "I can't thank you enough."

"Neither can I." Heather hugged Brian. "Thank you for bringing my mom home to me."

"You're welcome."

Fay put her arm around Heather as they walked up the stairs. When they got to the top, Madison was the first to hug her.

"I'm surprised to see you here." Fay walked into the kitchen, opened the refrigerator and took out a beer.

Madison's eyes filled with tears. "Our house is destroyed, gone."

"Oh my God. What happened?"

"The whole first floor got flooded out. Everything is gone."

"I am so sorry."

"Our house too, Mom. The water started gushing in."

"Are you telling me we lost everything?"

"I don't know. I left the house and came straight here."

"I want to go to the shop."

"Can't," Madison said. "The roads are all flooded out. It took us hours to get here."

"Same thing for me. We drove around like in a maze."

"Where's Shari?" Fay looked from Madison to Heather. "Something's going on. Do you care to fill me in on things?"

"Shari is in her bedroom. She had a fall. Winds up she broke her leg," Madison explained.

"Let me go see her."

"Wait." Madison grabbed her arm. "There's something we have to tell you before you walk into the living room."

"You two are scaring me."

"Hey, Shari would like a cup of coffee."

Fay turned around. Her mouth dropped open when she saw Benita standing there. "What the hell is she doing here? This bitch burned down my shop." With that Fay leaped at her.

"Someone help us," Heather screamed.

Tommy walked into the kitchen and separated the two ladies.

"What the hell are you two thinking?" Tommy asked.

"What I'm thinking is the woman who burned down my shop is standing in one of my best friend's house like she lives here."

"It's not what you think," Sophia said, appearing in the doorway.

"You could have fooled me."

"Shari will tell you why she let her stay here," Sophia said.

"*Por favor*," Benita said, "let me explain."

"I have nothing to say to you. You burned down my family store. No explanation is needed. You are..." Fay placed her beer down on the counter before sitting down in the kitchen chair.

"Are you all right, Mom?"

"I feel dizzy, a little confused." Fay covered her face with her hands. She counted backward from twenty. That's what the doctor in Italy told her to do when stressful situations like this happened. As soon as she got home, the worrying and running around got the best of her. She hadn't had any bouts with her memory the whole time she stayed in Italy.

"I can't let myself slip back into the place I was in when I left here. My time in Italy showed me my life shouldn't be filled with drama."

"I'm going to try my best not to let that happen," Madison said. "We will work with you. I promise we will all go to the store when we can get out of the area. I'm sure there is some merchandise we can save."

"I'm not worried about the store. I have a lot of things in my attic. I also sent Shari materials and other goodies from the bazaars in the back streets. I will rebuild. That will keep my mind fresh and alive." Fay stood. "I want to see Shari."

"She's in her bedroom."

As she walked through the living room, she greeted Dino with a hug.

"I'm sorry about the store. Tommy and I will help you. Don't worry."

"Thank you."

Fay walked down the short hall to Shari's bedroom. Shari sat on the bed with her left leg up on a pillow.

"Welcome back to complete chaos." Shari smiled. "I can't tell you how happy I am to see you. Come here, give me a hug."

Fay hugged her before sitting cross-legged on the bed. "I can't believe the mayhem going on here, starting with Benita. How could you bring her into your home after everything she has done to us?"

"Karma."

"What good can come from bringing her into your home?"

"I know what you mean. But when she showed up at my door, I knew she had nowhere else to go. I couldn't send her away. She was desperate."

"So was I. Nothing is like the feeling of not knowing if your daughter is alive after a severe hurricane. I sat in a bar at the airport in London watching all this go down on television, not being able to get a flight out of there."

Shari reached out to touch Fay's hand. "What Benita did to you is a terrible tragedy. Once I get this freakin' cast off my leg, I'll be out there helping you too. The one thing we have is each other. Benita is another of Angelo's victims. He promised her the world too."

Fay put her head down. "That bastard. He deserves to be in jail. I can't believe he still is rocking the boat from his jail cell."

Shari giggled. "Hopefully he is getting the pretty boy treatment."

"I sure hope so. Let him feel pain. But Benita," Fay pointed toward the living room, "I hate her. I could never forgive her for destroying everything."

"Maybe…" Shari stopped talking, her eyes closed as her head tilted from side to side.

Fay kept her eyes on her. She knew when Shari closed her eyes it meant she had drifted into her mind, making a connection to Fay through the bond of their friendship. No matter what Fay thought about, Shari always got deeper into her thought process, usually going to a place where she didn't share with anyone.

Fay waited patiently until Shari abruptly opened her eyes.

"What?" Fay asked as panic rose in her throat.

"It's all good. You will be thanking Benita in a few months."

Fay bit her bottom lip.

"Things will be hard the next few months." Shari lifted the deck of tarot cards and handed them to Fay. "You know the routine."

Fay knew the routine oh so well. Closing her eyes, she shuffled the cards over and over again. Just when she thought she should stop, something told her to keep going.

Normally, the cards slid in her hands like oil, giving off a dim energy. This time, the cards felt different. They felt like cotton. The energy of the cards radiated through her. Shari had always been right. The cards had always been right. *Scary.*

Fay handed the deck to Shari.

She fanned the cards on the bed.

"Close your eyes. Concentrate on your question. When you're ready pick a card. Pull the card out. Don't turn it over."

Fay closed her eyes. Her thoughts and questions were relating to her business. She had no idea what the store looked like or if there was anything left to salvage.

In her suitcases were her sketchbooks. Each day, she spent time on the stone terrace overlooking the small town in Sicily working on her designs. She wasn't looking to be a fashion designer. What she wanted to create were one-of-a-kind designs.

Opening her eyes, she gazed at Shari, nodding her head. Fay reached, scanned the seventy-two cards and stopped somewhere around the middle of the fan. She slid out the card.

"Are you sure?" Shari asked, her index finger on top of the card.

"Yes."

Shari turned the card over to reveal the *Death Card*.

Fay covered her mouth as she eyed the card. Slowly, she dropped her hands back into her lap.

"Wow. Right on the money." Shari smiled.

"I know." Fay sighed. "I don't know how you do it."

"You choose the card. I also saw in your face that you felt the positive energy the cards always bring to me."

"That was the first time I have truly felt the cards."

Shari rocked back and forth. "Would you mind fixing the pillow behind me? I think it's almost time for another painkiller."

"Want me to get one for you?"

"No. I want to address the card. Give me a few minutes to digest..."

While Shari closed her eyes, Fay kept her eyes fixed on the *Death Card*. The thirteenth card in the major arcana of the tarot card deck. A skeleton dressed in black sat on a white horse surrounded by people of all classes in society holding a black standard flag emblazoned with a white flower. In the background the sun was rising. The *Death Card* always scared her as it meant there would be some sort of change coming her way. But this time, she felt the complete opposite.

Fay raised her gaze to Shari. Slowly, Shari opened her eyes.

"Good things are coming your way. The store is your stepping stone. Heather is right when she said it's time to broaden your horizons. I see you letting go of the store. You are going to sell the building."

"I am?" Fay's eyebrows shot up. "I thought I would rebuild."

"You are, but not in the current location."

"Am I staying in Staten Island?"

"Yes. You are going to move your business to the south shore. You will continue to sell the vintage treasures you continue to pick up along the way. The difference is this time your own designs will be in the window. Many clients, a lot of work."

"What about love?"

"You will find love again. But your love of designing will be your relationship for the time being. Love will always be in your heart. However, you aren't ready to meet your next suitor. You will choose your business over love."

"Wow." Fay slid off the bed. She walked to the window and crossed her arms before turning around to face Shari. "I miss love, companionship. I can't believe I have two failed marriages. But I did meet someone in Sicily. I'm hoping he comes to visit me."

"He will. Be patient. Don't rush things." Squeezing her eyes shut, Shari bit her bottom lip and clenched her fists. "The pain is unbearable. I guess the painkiller from the hospital has worn off." She opened her eyes. "Can you hand me the pill bottle over on the dresser?"

Fay picked up the bottle and handed it to her. "You never told me what happened to your leg."

Shari popped a pill into her mouth, opened the bottle of green tea and took a slug. "When I opened the door, the wind slapped me in the face causing me to fall backward on my left leg."

"The spiral staircase?" Fay sat with her back to the headboard alongside Shari.

"That would be understandable. But no, I fell down the side stairs thinking I was going to go out and find Madison. The best part, I had to wait over a day for an ambulance to come to bring me to Brooklyn. The hospital here was evacuated."

"Oh dear God. What a nightmare. What did you break?"

"My ankle and fibula bone."

"Ouch."

"I'll more than likely be in a cast for over six weeks. Imagine I can't walk up the stairs to my altar room."

"Please, you'll hop up the stairs and come down with your leg straight ahead of you as you slide down on your butt."

They both looked at each other going hysterical.

"Stop making me laugh. The more I laugh, the more my leg hurts."

The doorbell rang, causing them to stop laughing.

"I'll get it." Fay heard Madison call out from the living room. "Hopefully that's Cassie."

"Go see what's going on. I'm really tired."

"I'll let you know who's here."

Fay got off the bed and returned to the living room. Madison walked back up the stairs with Scott behind her.

"Oh my God," Sophia yelled running into Scott's arms.

"Thank God you're fine. It took me hours to get back here. All the roads are closed. I couldn't get back onto Staten

Island. Then once I did, I drove around in circles. I refused to give up until I held you in my arms again."

Sophia stood on her toes so their lips met. Fay smiled. Maybe Gavino wasn't here with her at the moment, but she did have everything she needed for now.

"The only one missing now is Cassie," Madison said.

"And Antonio," Sophia mumbled between kisses.

Fay walked back into Shari's room. Shari was fast asleep. Walking over to the bed, she lifted the blanket off the bottom edge, placing it over Shari. Picking the *Death Card* really represented all of them. Each one of them had been affected by the hurricane. Taking a deep breath, she lost her train of thought.

Welcome home, Fay.

Chapter Fifteen

"We're almost there." Cassie pointed. "There's Shari's house on the next block. It's the house that is set back."

"Thank God. My feet are killing me."

"Ditto. My sneakers are now floating somewhere down on Hylan Boulevard." Cassie reached down to sweep her hand under her feet to remove the pieces of paper sticking to her heels.

"Disgusting. I never had black feet when I was a kid, nor have I ever walked out of my house without shoes on."

"Guess there's always a first time for everything." Crystal walked a few steps but stopped.

"I'm not sure what I'm going to do without Harris. He had become my whole life. After years of turning him down for dinner, I finally gave in. Our friendship turned into a beautiful affair." Tears escaped from Crystal's eyes. "Now, I don't know how I am going to live without him."

"I'll help you. Once we can get around, I will take you for therapy. We'll go through this together."

"Why would you want to help me? You just met me."

"My life has been crappy the past few years. I was always at an impasse. Every man I met since my divorce turned into a loser, until I met Antonio. Even with him, I don't open up all the way. I'm always afraid of getting hurt."

Crystal dried her eyes with her wet sweat shirt. "I think the hurt is the worst thing in life. When you have no one, there isn't anyone to hurt you." Crystal placed both hands on her head.

"I have to go to his parents, tell them what happened."

"You will when we can get out. It took us long enough to get here." Cassie reached her hand out. "Come on. Let's go to Shari's, get you into dry clothes and a pair of shoes. I don't know about you, but I sure as hell need a hot shower."

Crystal took her hand. "Thank you, Cassie. If it weren't for you, I probably would have ended my life. Your friendship means so much."

Cassie squeezed her hand. "Friends forever."

"I'd like that. I don't have many girlfriends. I never had the time. When I'm not taking classes, I'm working."

"Classes? I didn't know you were going to school."

"I decided to return to college to finish my degree. I wanted to join the police force, but I didn't have enough credits."

"I didn't know that. It's wonderful you're doing this."

"It is. But without Harris, well…I don't know if this is what I really want to do."

"You can't think about this. Right now we are in the middle of a crisis. Making any kind of decision now would be a huge mistake," Cassie said.

"I agree with you."

"Come on. We're almost there."

Cassie carefully walked down the block watching where she stepped. The past few blocks were perfectly fine. She couldn't believe a half a mile down the road the houses were totally destroyed, some being ripped right off their foundations.

The one thing she would never forget was the look on the peoples' faces at the shelter. Watching toddlers running around broke her heart. Hard to believe so many people were displaced from their homes. All the water had been the biggest surprise. The puddles were always in the same places, but the amount of water had been beyond puddles.

When she reached the salon's front door she sighed in relief. Her feet were throbbing. The last puddle they walked through, she stepped on a piece of metal that nicked her little toe. Her injury she kept to herself. No need to worry Crystal with such nonsense.

From outside, she could hear talking. The one voice she immediately recognized was Madison's. Her friend's voice was so distinct she could hear her in a crowd. With the palm of her hand, she rang the doorbell multiple times until she heard Madison yell, "Coming," before she stopped ringing.

The door flew open. Madison let out a scream before hugging her.

"I am so glad to see you. You were the last one we were waiting for."

"What are you talking about?"

"Everyone is here. Come on, let's go upstairs and get you out of those wet clothes. Poor Shari, we all took over her wardrobe." Madison giggled.

"I hope she has something for my friend, Crystal." Cassie stepped aside to reveal Crystal.

"Hell yeah." Madison reached her arms out. "Welcome." She hugged her too. "Where's Antonio?"

"He's down by the precinct helping out. So many people are displaced from their homes with their houses destroyed."

"I'm sure he'll come when he can."

Cassie walked up the stairs. By the time she reached the top, Sophia stood there waiting for her. The two cousins embraced. No words were exchanged. Just knowing she was alive made the ordeal of walking there worth it.

By the time she made it into the kitchen, there wasn't a dry eye in the room.

"I am so glad to see you," Fay said. "I can't tell you how happy I am all my friends are okay."

"What took you so long to get here?" Madison asked.

Cassie looked at Crystal who nodded her head. "We were stuck at the police precinct. Crystal's boyfriend died helping us."

"Oh no," Madison said covering her mouth.

"Antonio put us in a rowboat that brought us out to Bay Street, where we were then met by firemen who brought us to a Lutheran Church. They treated us like family. They gave us clean clothes and sneakers."

Madison's eyes traveled down to Cassie's feet, then Crystal's. "You're both barefooted. What the hell happened?"

"I lost my shoes in the last lake I swam through at the bottom of Quincy," said Crystal.

"They fell out of my hand into the water, or shall I say sewerage." Cassie held her hand up to her nose. "Don't even go there. I can't wait to get the hell out of these clothes. I hope you don't mind I brought Crystal with me."

"I'm sure Shari won't mind at all," Fay said. "Why not. If she let Benita stay here, why wouldn't she let Crystal?"

Cassie's eyes bulged opened. "Did you say Benita?"

"Yes. *The* Benita, who burned down my store and tried to destroy our lives."

"And Shari allowed this?" Cassie pivoted around on the balls of her feet. "Where the hell is Shari?"

"In her room. She's all right. But when she opened the front door, the wind pushed her against the stairs and she broke her leg."

"Oh dear God. That's terrible."

"She's lucky she didn't crack her head against the stairs," Madison explained.

"I'm going to see her. In the meantime, would you take care of Crystal, get her into dry clothes?"

"I'll be all right," Crystal said.

"Nonsense. We have gone through some heavy things the past twenty-four hours. I think you need to talk to Shari too," Cassie concluded. "Give me a few minutes with her. I will be right back."

Cassie walked through the living room and stopped when she saw Benita. She wanted to leap at her and wrap her hands around her neck. She had hurt every one of them, but somehow acting on her thoughts didn't seem worth it.

Walking down the hall, she stood outside Shari's bedroom door.

"Don't just stand there. Come on in." Shari sighed. "I can't tell you how relieved I am to finally know all my friends are safe."

Cassie sat on the edge of the bed. "It's been some hell of a day."

Shari pointed at her leg. "Tell me about it. But at least I know all my friends are together."

"Honestly, the whole ordeal has yet to settle into my mind. If it weren't for the grating in the goddamn ceiling, Antonio and I would have drowned."

"But you didn't."

"Yes, by the grace of God." Cassie gazed up at the ceiling. "I hope you don't mind I brought my friend Crystal with me. She lost her boyfriend last night."

"Oh, no. What happened?"

"I'll never forget the sound of the floor collapsing, along with the look on Antonio's face when he came into the room to tell Crystal her boyfriend died in the fall."

"Thank God you're okay. I have been reunited with all my friends with everyone being safely brought to me."

"You couldn't say it any better. You can't imagine how bad things are."

"The girls have told me as they arrived. I can't believe Father Capodanno Boulevard is a river, along with Hylan Boulevard in some places above Hylan."

"Do you have any cell phone service? I want to call my father, make sure him and Bruce are okay."

Shari lifted her cell phone off the bed and shook her head. "Still no service. Let me try the landline."

"You still have one of them?"

Shari reached over to her nightstand, lifting the cordless phone out of the cradle. "Yeah. Why? You don't?"

"I got rid of mine two years ago. I'm never home. Besides, the phone never rang anyway. Everyone calls me on my cell."

"Maybe you should think about getting one because," she handed her the phone, "I have a dial tone."

"No freakin' way." Cassie snatched the phone out of Shari's hand. She punched in the hotel's number. To her surprise the phone rang.

"Good evening, East Shore Hotel, Donika speaking, how may I help you?"

"Hi, Donika. Can I speak to Mr. Edwards?"

"I'm sorry, Mr. Edwards is busy. How can I help you?"

"This is Cassie Scott, his daughter. I need to speak to him for a couple of minutes. I'm sure he's expecting my call."

"Okay, hold on," she said in an annoyed tone.

Screw her. I have to make sure my dad is okay.

"Cassie?"

"Hi. Are you and Bruce all right?" she asked pacing in front of Shari's bed.

"Yes. Just going crazy. A lot of people have come here because their homes are flooded out. I have a full house here. It's so bad, people are sleeping on cots in the lobby."

"Oh shit, that's terrible."

"Are you okay? Where are you?"

Cassie had a hard time hearing him. In the background, she could hear kids screaming and people talking.

"I'm at Shari's."

"I hope you didn't get caught in the storm."

"No Dad, I didn't. I rode out the storm at Shari's," she lied. No way could she tell her dad about her ordeal. All he'd do is worry. He had enough on his plate, and didn't have to worry about something that had already happened.

"Stay put. From what I understand the streets are impassable all along the coastline. I don't need to worry about you along with the extra two hundred people stuffed into the lobby and conference rooms."

"Don't worry. I'm staying put. I'll make my way to the hotel when the roads clear up."

"Stay safe. We're okay over here. From what I'm seeing on television, it seems half the island is under water. I want you to stay in touch."

"I will, Dad."

"Call me later."

"I will unless we lose landline service again."

Cassie said her goodbyes before placing the phone on the bed. When her gaze met Shari's, she was surprised to see Shari smirking.

Cassie held open her hands. "What?"

"You finally called Harry, Dad." Shari squeezed her hand. "I am so proud of you."

"Hell, took me long enough to accept him and Bruce."

Harry had approached her while she was on a case, hiring her on the spot to find his son who he never met. After finding Bruce, she found out he was her half-brother, and was shocked by her mom's infidelity. Then when her mom got sick, Harry told her the truth, dropping yet another bombshell, that he was her biological father. Boy, how life threw her a curveball.

"Things are going to be all right," Shari said pushing the pillows up behind her. "Maybe you can give me a hand. I have another pillow in the closet." She pointed. "Can you please place it behind my neck?"

Cassie stood and grabbed the pillow off the shelf. "Tell me when you feel comfortable," she said placing it behind her neck.

"Up a few inches."

Cassie started moving the pillow again.

"Stop. Right there. Now I don't have to hold my head up straight. Hopefully the pain in my neck will stop for a bit." Shari took a deep breath. "Now I'm ready to do a ritual with you."

Cassie held up her hand. "Before you do any rituals, lighting of candles and shuffling of tarot cards, I need to know what the hell that woman is doing in your house."

"I've been waiting for you to ask." Shari nodded her head. "I'm going to tell you the same thing I told the others, she is here because of karma. I couldn't leave her wandering the streets with no place to go."

"There are plenty of shelters out there. Believe me, I know. I stopped in one of them. She burned down Fay's store. Isn't that enough to warrant her being out on the street?"

"Yes it is. But you should know better than that. Benita is a victim too."

"Maybe you can forgive and forget, but I can't. However, I will respect your decision."

"Thank you."

Cassie dropped her hands to her hips. "But she is not welcome to our ritual."

"No, she isn't. Nor is your friend Crystal. They are outsiders. We need to be together to seal our circle." Shari picked up her deck of tarot cards. "Please get the girls."

* * * *

When Cassie left the room, Shari repositioned herself on the bed, leaving enough room for the girls to sit around. She tried to get hold of the velvet bag of candles on the nightstand, the ones Heather had brought to her right after her fall, but she couldn't reach it.

Madison came in first, with a cup of green tea with a twist of lime, along with a dish of chocolate biscottis.

"Thanks," Shari said taking the mug from Madison. "I can use your help."

"Tell me what you need."

"I can't reach the velvet bag of candles on the nightstand. Can you set them up on the breakfast tray, this way I can put the tray over my legs?"

Without hesitating, Madison stood, placed the white candle in the middle and placed five small candles around the center one, before sitting next to her.

Shari started shuffling the cards from hand to hand. "Are the others coming?"

"In a few minutes. I asked them to give me a few minutes with you."

"Is everything all right?" Shari asked taking Madison's hand in hers.

"Yes. Everything is fine. Dino is fine. Dino is so fine that we got trapped in the crawl space." Madison giggled. "I can't believe I got my husband back."

Shari knew exactly what she meant. Leave it to Madison to get caught in her crawl space because she was having sex. The authorities would crucify her if they found out the reason why they didn't evacuate. But her best friend was fine. Everything would be fine, but somewhat different.

"I'm so happy for you."

"Thanks." Madison pointed to Shari's leg in a cast. "I'm just sorry you broke your leg, coming to find me. I'll tell you one thing, first chance I get to call the cell phone company I'm going to insist on a credit."

"Not worth it. The bottom line is we're here together." Shari reached out to Madison. They joined hands. "You're my best friend. We have gone through a lot together. We will always be blood sisters."

"Yes we will."

"Knock, knock," Cassie sang, standing at the door. "Can we come in?"

Shari waved them in. "This is going to be a little uncomfortable, different from our usual ritual. Because," she pointed to her leg, "I can't sit cross-legged."

"Not to worry. We'll squeeze in on the bed," Fay said.

"Cassie, before you sit, can you shut the door?"

Cassie pushed the door closed before joining the others.

"We're going to start by all holding hands."

Shari took Madison and Fay's hands. The energy in the room, priceless. Even though each of them had gone through an ordeal, each of them had a positive outlook on their experience.

"We are all gathered here today in celebration," Shari began, "alive and all making it through the horrible tragedy that has taken place. Our circle is still strong. Nothing will ever destroy the friendship we have built." Shari let go of Madison and Fay's hand and lit the tall wooden match before lighting the candle in the middle. "Please watch over us, keep us together, no matter where life leads us." Once the candle was lit, Shari reached out to take Madison and Fay's hand.

Shari felt Madison's energy. Madison was pumped. Her husband was back, however, the future of their home and business left her at an impasse.

"Don't make yourself crazy, Madison," Shari said. "Sure things are going to be tough in the beginning. You'll be fighting everyday with the insurance company until you write an article for the newspaper. It's after that you will get the

Karen Cino

restitution you deserve. Be very wary of your decisions. Think twice before jumping in. Do what's best for you and Dino." Shari squeezed Madison's hand. "And don't let anyone persuade you into doing anything you don't want to do. Make all your decisions with Dino as a team. You will be fine after a bit of a struggle. So mote it be."

Madison's eyebrows shot up. "Struggle?"

"Yes. But don't dwell on it." Shari motioned to Madison with her chin.

Madison lifted the wooden match off the table and lit the small white candle. "So mote it be."

"Before we go on, I must tell you that each one of us has a rocky road ahead of us. Things aren't going to be smooth. We will all struggle in different ways, but will achieve our goals, in time."

Shari looked around her circle. Her friends all sat with different concerns. She decided to try her best to keep a positive twist on what she told them. No sense in worrying them when, in the end, the outcome would be positive.

Next, she squeezed Fay's hand. "You have had a streak of bad luck. You are devastated about your store. But in reality, the fire is the best thing that could have happened to you. Your struggle with the onset of early Alzheimer's will be put in remission. Your dream of being a designer is just around the corner."

"It is?"

"Every design in your sketchbook is amazing."

"I didn't show you..."

Shari ignored her. "The dresses are spectacular along with the material you'll be using. Take a negative, turn it into a positive. You will rebuild. Do not get rid of the glass counter showcase. Tommy will strip the wood, stain it. This way you are bringing a piece of the past into the future."

"We'll model and promote your designs," Cassie said. "I'm sure the girls won't mind wearing them."

"Not at all," Madison said. "I'm going to need a new wardrobe after losing most of my clothes."

"We're all here to help you," Sophia added. "Since becoming a part of this circle, I have grown emotionally. I'll be honored to wear your designs."

Tears rolled down Fay's cheeks. "I'm so lucky to have such wonderful friends."

"We will all be there for you. Well, maybe not me." Shari pointed at her leg. "But you know I'll give you all the emotional support you need. So mote it be."

Fay lit the candle. "So mote it be."

Shari sighed. Closing her eyes, she knew down the road these get-togethers wouldn't be happening on a regular basis. But for now, they were all here. This, her house, was the place they would always come back to when things got rough. That's why tonight, would always be special to them.

Shari opened her eyes, directing her gaze to Cassie. "You keep getting thrown one curve ball after another. This time, things will be different. You have finally found a man who adores you for you. Yes there will be bumps in the road, but both of you will come to a compromise. Stay open to his ideas. Don't shut them down."

"What kind of ideas?" Cassie asked, her gaze not leaving Shari's.

"Living arrangement, work environment. Keep an open ear and open arms for his kids. You have a wonderful life ahead of you. Don't compare. Remember everyone has their own personality and quirks. Go beyond them. Life will be wonderful. So mote it be."

Cassie picked up the wooden match in front of her. Slowly, she took the flame from the middle candle to light her own. "So mote it be," she whispered before blowing out the match and placing it in front of Sophia.

Shari reached for her mug of tea. She took a sip and placed it back down on the nightstand. Looking toward Sophia, she could see the fear in her eyes. Shari knew she felt uncomfortable at these get-togethers. She would never reveal Sophia's deep dark secrets in front of everyone or breathe a word of her past. It was up to her to share that part of her life.

"Sophia, you have been through one of the worst ordeals of your life, yet you are sitting here with us, alive and well with a drop dead gorgeous professional athlete sitting in the other room. You have some things to work through, as does Scott. He will be making a huge, life changing decision regarding his career in the upcoming weeks and will need your support. Things are going to be okay. You just need to brush off the negative energy, open up your heart. So mote it be."

Sophia didn't say a word. Instead she started rocking back and forth. Everyone remained quiet, waiting for her to light the last candle. Shari knew why. Sophia worried about the box of letters that she didn't have a chance to burn in the fire. But she had nothing to worry about. She would get to them before anyone saw them.

Cassie placed her arm around Sophia's shoulder. With her other hand, she lifted the wooden match to place in Sophia's hand.

"Thank you," Sophia whispered.

Reaching the long match to the white candle in the middle, she lit the end and then her candle. She held the lit match in her hand for a few seconds before blowing it out. "So mote it be."

"Now that we have all lit our candles, it's safe to say we are bonded together as sisters. We will always be a part of each other's lives, no matter where we are in our lives. So what I'd like for all of you to do is sign my cast." Shari opened her nightstand drawer and took out a box of colored magic markers.

"Hiding the markers?" Madison asked.

"Of course. Anything left out is community property." Shari giggled. "I'm going to sit back and let you girls decorate this ugly white cast."

Shari watched her friends go to work. She was exactly where she wanted to be at this time in her life. God had been good to her. She had been blessed with a great husband, beautiful son along with a set of friends many would die for.

No matter what happened moving forward, they would all survive, remaining friends for life. So mote it be.

Epilogue

A year later…

Shari slid the leaf into the dining room table while Tommy went out to the garage to get the folding table. This would be the first time in a year they were all together. She had insisted on doing all the cooking.

Once Thomas went to school all day, she had more time on her hands. She had kept her regular customers and hired another beautician to cut hair, freeing up two of her days. Helping Thomas with his homework had turned into a part-time job. The school projects were endless.

Tommy had been so busy since the hurricane. His business had quadrupled causing him to hire another assistant, so he had some time to spend with her and Thomas.

"Damn, everything smells awesome." Tommy took her in his arms for a hug and a kiss. "You did a great job. I know you're excited about spending time with your friends, especially Madison."

"I am. I talk to her everyday, but it isn't the same as her daily stop bys for a cup of coffee and a bagel. Because of her, I pull out the dough in a bagel and Italian bread, except for Sundays when I make a pot of gravy. When I dip the Italian bread in the gravy, I need to have the whole thing."

"I hear you on that. Nice habit we picked up from your best friend." Tommy pulled the legs of the table open and placed the table next to the dining room table. Now the table extended the whole length of the living room.

"Thank you." Shari kissed him. "Before you sit down in front of the television, I need you to help me with one more thing."

Tommy looked at his watch. "You have nine minutes before the game begins."

"Thanks." She giggled. "I know the football game is going on, meaning you guys will be on the couch."

"What's the difference, babe? You'll be up in your room with your friends."

Shari took one of the tablecloths off the counter and placed it on the kitchen table. "I hope you don't mind keeping an eye on Thomas for a while," she said covering the folding table with a matching tablecloth.

Tommy chuckled. "You didn't even have to ask. I have you covered."

Shari spun around in her stocking feet to face Tommy. Reaching out, she put her arms around his neck. "I love you so much." Tommy's arms stretched around her waist. "I wish we had time to squeeze a quickie in. Where's Thomas?"

"He's in his room watching cartoons."

Shari swayed her hips against him feeling his hardness. "Let's quietly go into the bathroom. I need to check your pipes."

* * * *

Madison made sure all the windows were closed and locked before heading downstairs. On the top of the bookcase opposite the potbelly stove, sat small picture frames filled with group shots of her and the girls. In the middle was a picture of Shari and her. Madison smiled. She missed her friend. She hated not being able to jump in her car to drive over to her shop whenever she wanted.

After the hurricane, Dino and her stayed with Shari until the inspector went through their house. The damage had been beyond repair. Their whole house was filled with mold. They spent weeks cleaning out the house. Dino's studio had been wiped out along with the first floor of their house. Upstairs, the items of clothes left on the shelves or hanging remained unmarred. In total, Madison had only been able to save two suitcases of clothes, including shoes and a couple of handbags. Plus a few boxes of memories from the crawl space attic.

That night they had both wept. Their whole life had been washed away by the storm. The decision to move was a hard one. Madison didn't want to leave her friends in Staten Island, but to rebuild their house would cost them more than moving. Since the houses around theirs were also destroyed, a contractor came in and offered them a good price on the property. After careful consideration, they decided to accept the offer. In the past, they had discussed moving to Pennsylvania. The reality of buying another house in Staten Island would mean taking out a mortgage, something neither one of them wanted to do since they had already paid off the house they had lost.

Dino suggested they spend a few days in Milford, Pennsylvania to get a feel of small town living. Reluctant at first, Madison kept her concerns to herself going along with Dino. To her surprise, she fell in love with the small town.

The people were friendly, the houses old-fashioned with potbelly stoves, fireplaces and wrap around porches.

They found a two-story house with a cottage in the back. Madison wouldn't call it a cottage though. Its size was that of the first floor of her old house. Dino walked around the cottage like a little kid in a candy store talking about where he would put all his equipment and how he would soundproof the room. The excitement in his voice and actions sold Madison. At this point in her life, she had to think about what was best for them. A laid-back environment like this would be perfect for Dino, keeping him stress free. The shopping left a lot to be desired, but Madison could stock up on clothes when she visited Shari.

Madison locked the front door. She walked around the back of the house on the slate path to the cottage where Dino worked.

Since they moved to Milford, Dino's business had bloomed. The musicians loved that they could come and spend a week in the guest bedroom in the cottage while working on their recordings with Dino.

Madison kept busy by working on their emagazine that had become a huge success. Companies constantly emailed her asking for space in Rockin' On. Madison had a staff that worked out of their houses all over the country. With a staff, Madison had some free time, during which she secretly started working on a novel.

She opened the door. "Hey, are you ready?"

Dino twirled around in the high back fully padded office chair and stood. "Waiting for you."

"I locked everything up, packed everything in the back seat and have the thermal coffee mugs ready for our journey back home in the car."

Dino's left eyebrow rose. "Baby, we are home."

"I know." Madison reached her hand out to Dino before crushing her body into his. "Just for the record, I couldn't be any happier in my life than I am at this moment. It's just hard not calling Staten Island home."

Dino ran his fingers through her hair, kissing the top of her head. "These past few months have been the best of my life. I miss the city life too. But being here with you, I feel as if we are making up for lost time."

"I wouldn't trade my life for anything. I love you so much."

"Me too. Now let's get going before I take you back into the house."

Madison backed out of his embrace. "Don't make promises you can't keep," she said walking outside.

"Don't worry, I won't."

He followed Madison into their Land Rover and slid behind the driver's seat. The moment Madison reached for the radio, Dino slapped her hand.

"Remember, whoever drives has radio control."

"Oh, come on. Are we going to go through this again?" Madison folded her arms, extending out her bottom lip.

"How about first hour my music, second hour classic rock?"

"Now that's a plan."

* * * *

Fay glanced at her watch, happy she still had time to straighten up the store before she had to leave for Shari's. Everything had changed since the day of the hurricane. But Shari was right. Things had turned out even better. The money she received for the old store, she had used to purchase another building on the south shore. She took Shari's advice having Tommy restore the glass showcase, the only thing from the old store that wasn't destroyed.

The fire had destroyed all the clothes and jewelry. Her house too had taken a beating. Three and a half feet of water had covered the first floor. The damage was repairable, however, she decided not worth the effort. She sold her house, moving a few blocks away from her store in the town of Princess Bay.

Seven months later, she launched her clothing line with Heather's help. The storm had brought them closer together. They worked as a team. Fay even taught Heather how to sew. She created her designs with the fabric she'd sent home from Sicily, while Heather set up the store. The grand opening had been an even bigger surprise. Not only did most of her designs sell out, but she'd received orders for more.

Earlier she had received an order for jewelry and scarves that she wanted to put out before she left. But first, she wanted to box the dresses she had made for her friends. Everyone she handmade was one-of-a-kind made especially for each of them. This would be her way of thanking them. Her friends had helped her clean out her house, boxed up all the things on the second floor and throw out everything on the first.

This was a new beginning for her. She had finally achieved her dream of being a fashion designer. Everyone loved her designs. She had plenty of orders to keep her busy for a long time.

The last trip to the doctor went well. He had said her early onset of Alzheimers seemed to be in remission. Keeping herself busy and taking her medication had worked miracles, along with her prayers to Saint Anthony.

After she packed the dresses, she unpacked the new merchandise before placing it in the glass counter. In the beginning, she'd tried to duplicate the look of her old store. Heather insisted they go for a more modern look, with the glass showcase being the core of the shop. At first she'd been hesitant, but gave in. Best decision she had ever made. Her daughter was following in her footsteps.

"Mom, are you almost ready?" Heather asked standing by the office door.

"Yes. I'm just going to put the new merchandise away in the showcase."

"Okay, but don't take too long. We still have to go home and pop the pies in the oven to bring to Aunt Shari's."

"I'll only be another twenty minutes."

"Perfect. That will give me enough time to finish putting in an order."

Fay looked up, pushing her bifocals up on her forehead. "Did you call Rosalina and ask her to send me more black and white material?"

"Yes. She's sending it out today FedEx. She also says she is sending you some other material along with the shoes you wanted." Heather rested her hands on her hips. "Shoes, Mom?"

"Yes." Fay dropped her bifocals back onto her nose. "A woman never has enough shoes. Besides, I thought it would be cool to showcase some of the shoes in the window."

"You're such a girly girl." Heather laughed. "That's why all my friends love you so much."

Fay grinned. Life couldn't be any better.

* * * *

"Are you almost ready to leave?" Cassie asked Antonio while putting her files in a pile.

"Almost. I just about finished the paper work from earlier. I hate when I make an arrest right before the end of my shift."

"Don't worry. We still have time. We'll stop for the beer and wine on the way to Shari's."

"Are you still working?" Antonio asked.

"Not really. While I'm waiting for you, I figured I'd catch up on some of this paper work."

"I'll meet you downstairs in the lobby, let's say in about a half-hour."

"Works for me."

Cassie hung up the phone. She sat back in her chair playing with the huge diamond and matching wedding band on her finger. She couldn't believe they had already been married close to ten months. When Antonio proposed to her, he shocked her. She never expected him to give her such a beautiful diamond ring. The next day, they went down to city hall, filled out the paper work and got married with Antonio's kids, Bruce and her dad in attendance.

They honeymooned in the Virgin Islands where they made the decision to live in Cassie's—thankfully undamaged—house. When they returned home, Cassie received an offer for a position as a consultant with her own office at the police precinct. She continued her private investigation practice, but spent a great deal of time doing process serving for the police. When she did work on her own cases, she'd go to Shari for help.

Antonio had another two years left before he retired. He wanted to move down to a warmer climate where they could enjoy outdoor activities all year long. Cassie had agreed. She could see her friends anytime she wanted to. Wherever they moved, she knew they'd only be a car drive away. Antonio would never move too far away from his kids. But things could change in two years, just the way things changed in a matter of a couple of hours the night of the biggest hurricane in over a hundred years.

* * * *

Sophia zipped up the black leather boots Scott had surprised her with earlier. With the baseball season over, Scott spent most of the day home. Making the decision to retire from playing had been a hard one for him. But within two hours of his retirement, he had been offered a job as pitching coach, which meant he would still be involved in the game.

When Sophia wasn't working at the catering hall or making centerpieces, she volunteered at Midland Beach bringing food to the homeless. As the weeks turned into months, Sophia was thrilled when Scott wasn't on the road with the team. Now with the season over, she cherished the time they spent together.

Max sat on her bed watching her. She couldn't help but sit down and push the cat on his back to kiss his stomach. If she hadn't found Max, she wouldn't have met Scott.

Scott had planned to move in with her the day of the hurricane. However, the hurricane delayed that. By the time Scott arrived at Shari's, her house had already turned into a fraternity. The streets were blocked off and most of Staten Island didn't have electricity. Shari only had lights because her block had been hooked up to the backup generator for the bridge. They didn't make it back to Sophia's apartment until two days later. Scott had been so thankful to Shari and Tommy for letting them stay that he thanked them by giving them a vacation in the Caribbean, offering their services to take care of Thomas.

Once things calmed down a bit, they went to Allentown so Scott could visit his aunts and pick up more of his belongings. While he packed at his house, Sophia went to hers where she went up into the closet and took down the two boxes of letters. This time, she didn't open them. Instead, she threw them into the fire pit in the backyard, setting them ablaze.

Sophia stood over the fire pit watching them burn. That part of her life would always remain in her past. Scott loved her. He didn't have to know about her years of uncertainty and how she almost took her life. Finally, after all these years, she could honestly say she was at peace with herself.

When the letters turned to ashes, she returned to the house. Walking around the living room, she lifted a few knickknacks that reminded her of her aunt off the mantel and cocktail table. Carefully, she wrapped them in paper towels before placing them in a tote bag.

"Sophia?" Scott's voice echoed into the living room.

"I'm in the kitchen wrapping up a few things to give to Cassie."

Scott appeared in her kitchen wearing the blue-mirrored glasses he had on when he saved her by pulling over to the side of the road, the first day she held Max as a kitten. He removed his sunglasses and slid one of the arms of the glasses down the front of his black T-shirt.

"I'm done over at my place. I closed everything up in the house. Is there anything you need help with?"

Sophia gazed into Scott's ocean blue eyes, getting lost in them. They decided to keep both their houses in Allentown for the time being. Scott sold his condo in Manhattan. He suggested she keep her apartment in Staten Island for when the team played at home. What he wanted was for the two of them to live up in Allentown in her house during the off-season. She'd agreed to think about it. Even considering leaving her job was a big step. She loved making centerpieces and favors. After talking to her boss, he agreed she could continue working at home. She signed a new contract and already had enough work for the next seven weeks.

"Nope, I got everything ready."

"Do you want me to cover the furniture?" he asked lifting the covers off the metal rack in the corner.

"That won't be necessary."

Scott placed the blanket back in the rack. "Why?"

"Because it's the winter. The off-season. I'll pack a few clothes from the apartment. Tomorrow morning we can come back home."

"Are you sure?" he asked pulling her closer to him.

"Yes."

Scott took her face in his hands, leaned down and kissed the top of her head. As she gazed into his eyes, she knew for the first time in her life she had made the right decision.

* * * *

Madison and Dino drove down Father Capodanno Boulevard on the way to Shari's. Most of the devastation remained the same. Some homes were rebuilt, while others still stood abandoned with red stickers from the city on the front door. Another shock had been the amount of for sale signs on the homes. Folding tables and tents had remained in designated areas to feed residents who lost everything.

"I can't look at this anymore. It's so depressing. I'm going to take the back streets to Shari's."

"Maybe we can pass our old house, see what the contractor did with it?"

"Are you sure?" he asked, when he stopped at the stop sign. "Do you think you can handle seeing the house without crying?"

"Yes. I am happy and content with where we are."

Dino made a left. People were still removing water-soiled items from their homes. People were still rebuilding. He stopped in front of their old house.

Madison opened the car door and walked up the walkway. At the door, she turned the doorknob. The door was unlocked.

"Babe, I don't think you should go in there," he said following behind.

Ignoring him, Madison walked into the house. Everything looked exactly the way they left it. She headed to the back of the house into Dino's studio. All his equipment remained the way the hurricane left it.

Madison shook her head, as tears rolled down her cheeks. "Horrible."

Dino took her hand. "Come on. Let's get out of here. This is our past. We have built an empire in Milford."

"Yes, we have. Together."

The rest of the ride to Shari's they sat in silence. Some businesses had reopened, while others remained abandoned. When they pulled up in front of Shari's, before she even got out of the car, the girls were all standing outside waiting for her.

Madison swung the car door open and rushed out of the car.

She hugged each one of them. "I can't believe we are all together. You all look great."

"So do you," Shari said with the others all agreeing.

"I'm going to watch the game while you all do your girly giggling thing out here." Dino chuckled.

After Dino walked inside, Shari lifted her arms and held them out. "Let's all join hands."

"Out here?" Fay asked.

"Yes."

The girls all stood in a circle, holding hands as if they were going to sing Ring Around the Rosy.

"We are all here together today to celebrate our friendship. Even though we are all at different places in our lives, we are still bonded together in spirit. We are all happy in our own way. I suggest we do this at least twice a year so we can all renew our friendship. Do we all agree?"

"Yes." They nodded their heads.

"We have all found it in our hearts to forgive Benita for the chaos she made of our lives. She will find happiness back home in the Dominican Republic."

They all shook their heads in agreement.

"I'd like to thank you all for coming today with open arms and open hearts. Today is the beginning of a new cycle in our lives. Madison, Fay, Cassie, Sophia, you will all be rewarded with happiness in your lives. We will continue to be united by our friendship and love. So mote it be."

"So mote it be," they all chanted together before another group hug.

The End

About the Author

Karen Cino is an author, poet and former journalist. She'd been writing since she was fourteen years old. She started her career by writing poetry, short stories and articles for her high school newspaper and the Staten Island Register. After reading Jackie Collin's "Lovers and Gamblers" she knew she found her niche, writing women's fiction.

Her daily walk down at the boardwalk is what gets her muse going. It clears her mind and helps her find realistic plot ideas and characters, boosting her muse. She loves writing about local places that people can relate to.

Karen is a single mom living in Staten Island, New York with her two adult children, Michael and Nicole, and three cats.

Website: www.karencino.com
Blog: www.karencinobooks.com

Secret Cravings Publishing

www.secretcravingspublishing.com

Manufactured by Amazon.com
Columbia, SC
03 April 2017